"You didn't answer my question," I told Carrina.

She looked at me. "What question?"

"Where have you been?" I repeated.

Carrina smiled. "Right here."

"But where?" I asked. "We don't go to the same school, or I would have seen you. Where is your family? Who are your friends?" I wanted to know everything.

Carrina tucked a strand of long, brown hair behind her ear. "My two best friends are in the Year Abroad program this year. One is in London, the other in Paris."

"What a coincidence," I said. "My school is hosting a student in the Year Abroad program—an American." I started laughing. "I heard she went into the boys' bathroom today."

I expected Carrina to laugh. Instead her face turned red as though she were embarrassed. I shook my head. "So typically American, to go to a foreign country where you don't know the language, to expect everyone to cater to you and put up signs in English. I hope my path crosses hers someday just so I can tell her how silly I think she is."

She looked like she might be ill. "Excuse me, will you?"

I watched her hur
wait to get away from

D0802842

Love Stories

Year Abroad Trilogy

Rome: Antonio & Carrie

RACHEL HAWTHORNE

BANTAM BOOKS
NEW YORK • TORONTO • LONDON • SYDNEY • AUCKLAND

In loving memory of my dad.

RL: 6, AGES 012 AND UP

ROME: ANTONIO & CARRIE
A Bantam Book / November 2000

Cover photography by Michael Segal.

Copyright © 2000 by 17th Street Productions,
an Alloy Online, Inc. company, and Jan Nowasky.
Cover art copyright © 2000 by 17th Street Productions,
an Alloy Online, Inc. company.

All rights reserved. No part of this book may be reproduced or transmitted
in any form or by any means, electronic or mechanical, including
photocopying, recording, or by any information storage and retrieval
system, without permission in writing from the publisher.
For information address Bantam Books.

 Produced by 17th Street Productions,
an Alloy Online, Inc. company.
33 West 17th Street
New York, NY 10011.

If you purchased this book without a cover you should be aware
that this book is stolen property. It was reported as "unsold and
destroyed" to the publisher and neither the author nor the pub-
lisher has received any payment for this "stripped book."

ISBN: 0-553-49328-0

Visit us on the Web! www.randomhouse.com/teens

Published simultaneously in the United States and Canada

Bantam Books is an imprint of Random House Children's Books, a
division of Random House, Inc. BANTAM BOOKS and the rooster
colophon are registered trademarks of Random House, Inc. Bantam Books,
1540 Broadway, New York, New York 10036.

PRINTED IN THE UNITED STATES OF AMERICA

OPM   0 9 8 7 6 5 4 3 2 1

One

Carrie

BUZZING ALONG THE bustling street on a borrowed Vespa scooter, I had an incredibly strong urge to shout, *Ciao! Everyone, look at me! I'm here at last!*

Here was the most awesome of cities: Rome. The Eternal City. As I wove in and out of traffic, I, sixteen-year-old Carrie Giovani, felt like I'd come home. But home was really Mustang, Texas. A little town on the far side of nowhere. My mother had grown up there, and unfortunately, so had I. Not that I disliked Mustang. My best friends—Robin Carter and Dana Madison—lived there. We were constantly together. My oldest brother, Marcus, referred to us as The Three Stooges, but I always thought of us as The Three Musketeers—always willing to embrace adventure.

But I digress. In Mustang, I worked in my dad's pizzeria. I enjoyed school, was popular, and got the leading roles in school plays. But a part of me had wanted more. Something deep inside me had always longed for the romance of Rome. I'm not talking kissy-face romance here. I'm talking grandeur, history, art, and vibrant people who know how to enjoy life.

Rome. The city where my father had been born and raised. He'd told me once that in his youth, he'd been restless. I could certainly relate to that feeling. I always wanted to go places, do things, be in the center of it all. Absolutely no sidelines for me.

I figured that my mom must have had a bit of a restless streak in her as well. She'd gone to Europe during the summer after her graduation from college. She'd met my dad while she was touring Rome. And the rest, as they say, is history. They fell in love. He'd proposed marriage before she returned to Mustang. They'd had what gossip columnists discussing Hollywood types always refer to as a whirlwind courtship.

Pretty romantic, huh?

I always thought so. Anyway, my dad said goodbye to his family and immigrated to the States. He moved to Mustang, married my mom, and established Giovani's Pizzeria. The business thrived, but not to the extent that he'd been able to afford to take his family of seven children to Italy. But many a night he told us about his homeland, and I fell in love with a place I'd never visited.

Now I was here, puttering along those very streets, waving at people I didn't know. Grinning like a fool—a fool in love with all that surrounded her. I couldn't have been happier or more excited. I believed that the whole world was a stage and that we should play as many roles as we can. Daughter. Student. Friend. Waitress—my least favorite role. Explorer. Adventurer was my latest, greatest role. Of course, I didn't know any of the scenes yet, and all my lines were ad-lib. No rehearsals. It was sort of like being an improv actress.

I was going to attend a school in Rome for an entire year. I'd been accepted into the Year Abroad program—just like my two best friends. Dana was spending the year in Paris. Her goal was to find a cute French guy to romance her. Robin was spending the year in London with one incredibly hot host brother, Kit Marlin. I'd met him during a one-day layover in London. I'd considered changing places with her, but with five older brothers in Mustang, I was looking forward to a year without guys hogging the bathroom and the television. My host sister, Elena Pietra, was an only child. In her home I would have peace and quiet—and a bedroom all to myself. No sharing with my younger sister, Maria.

Like my friends, I had a goal for the year: to get in touch with my Italian side. To become one with my heritage. Not that I was far from that goal. I had long, dark hair and an olive complexion. In Mustang, I stood out as an Italian. But I knew that there really wasn't an Italian "look" to speak of. People in northern Italy tended to be fair, those in the south dark. But as I sped along the *via*—the street—I saw blondes *and* brunettes.

I knew I'd fit in here. I had the added advantage of speaking Italian fluently. So fluently, in fact, that in my mind I always heard English when anyone spoke Italian. My mind was simply set for automatic translate. Back in Mustang, my dad spoke Italian, my mom English. Yet I never got confused. Like a heavy-duty sponge, I simply absorbed both languages. When I spoke English, I had a Texas drawl, and when I spoke Italian, it was pure Italian. I could, when the situation warranted, even speak English with an Italian accent—something that had impressed my hometown when I had played Juliet in our school's production of *Romeo and Juliet*. After all, fair Verona was in Italy. Of course, our Romeo had spoken his lines with a bit of a twang . . . but his failure had only served to make my star shine more brightly.

I figured my fluency in Italian was going to come in handy this year. I'd been with Dana when she'd bought her English-French dictionary. She had taken French for two years at Mustang High but wasn't taking any chances. I didn't need an English-Italian dictionary. As a matter of fact, once my plane had touched down in Rome yesterday and my host sister had met me at the airport, I hadn't spoken a single word of English.

I had become totally immersed in Italy! Tomorrow

I would become immersed in an Italian school. But right now it was time to become immersed in family. I'd suggested staying with my aunt and uncle for my year in Italy, but my parents had thought the familiarity of family would take away from the experience of living in a foreign country with people I didn't know.

I'd promised my father that I would visit his sister as soon as I got settled in. Aunt Bianca and her family owned a restaurant. I'd looked it up in my guidebook. Yes, as much as I knew about Rome, I didn't know everything. A guidebook was a must for a girl who came from a town so small that you could see all of it just by driving down Main Street.

I had been pleased to discover that my aunt's restaurant wasn't that far away. I'd borrowed Elena's Vespa scooter—or, as most Italians referred to it: her wasp. It sounded like a bee buzzing along the street, but it was the easiest way to get around. Rome's streets were narrow and crowded. Plus the city had been built on seven hills. Riding a bicycle was out of the question for me—I hadn't ridden a bike since I was ten. There was also no way that I was going to risk driving a car. The Italians were lethal! They loved their little cars and sped along the streets pretty much like maniacs. Everyone had a cell phone because they were more reliable than the regular phone service, and everyone talked on the phone when they drove. And it was no myth that Italians talked with their hands; here they were, holding the cell phone with one hand, gesturing wildly with the other—and what was holding the steering wheel? A pair of knees, maybe? I didn't know. Didn't want to know. I just knew that it made me nervous. Slow traffic and congestion were also rampant. Another reason that the scooters were so popular. I could weave in and out of the stalled or stopped vehicles.

The Eternal City had recently been cleaned of pollution, the buildings scrubbed down until they revealed their original colors. Every now and then I saw a small electric bus humming along. I guessed the improvements were all part of Rome's desire to be shiny for the new millennium.

I finally arrived at my destination. I read the words engraved on the stone building: *La Sera*. Evening. I thought that name was romantic. It was my aunt Bianca and uncle Vito Romano's trattoria. A trattoria was a family-owned restaurant with good home cooking. A *ristorante* was usually more elegant and much more expensive. On either side of the door of the trattoria was a mosaic of clouds, stars, and a moon. Mosaics were very popular in Italy and adorned many of the buildings that I'd passed. I hadn't seen any yet, but I'd heard that mosaics often decorated the floors as well.

I brought the Vespa to a halt and moved it to the side of the building, where several others were already parked. I figured most belonged to the employees. Patrons would no doubt show up at this nice establishment in a cab.

I removed my helmet and pulled the red scrunchie out of my hair to release my ponytail. My brown hair fell like a curtain past my shoulders. I ran my fingers quickly through the thick strands. I was going to meet my father's sister and her family for the first time. I wanted to make a good impression, but I didn't want to overdo it, or I'd have something to live up to the next time we visited. I figured it was best just to be me.

The Romanos lived in an apartment above the restaurant. I climbed the stairs, my heart pounding. This moment was the most exciting of my life. I was going to meet the woman my father had probably teased while he was growing up. Taking a deep breath, I knocked on the heavy oak door.

It flew open as though the woman standing in the portal had been waiting for me. She was well-rounded, her black hair streaked with silver pulled up into a bun on top of her head. Her cheeks puffed out as she smiled broadly and held out her arms. "Carrina!"

"Aunt Bianca!" I stepped into her hearty embrace. Carrina is my real name, but only my dad calls me that—and my mom when I've done something wrong. To the rest of the world, I'm Carrie. But I loved the way my name rolled off her tongue in such a rich Italian accent.

She took my arms and pushed me back a little. "I would know you anywhere," she said in halting English. "You look just like your papa." Actually, except for the coloring, I looked mostly like my mom—but if she wanted to see her brother in me, hey, that was fine. I knew my father had sent them school pictures and family photos every year. And they had done the same, sending us family photos that included their five sons. So I felt like I was meeting someone I already knew, for the most part. Still, seeing someone in the flesh made it all the more real.

She beckoned me inside. "Come, meet the rest of the family."

The living room was quite small—or maybe it just seemed small with six guys standing in its center. Uncle Vito looked exactly like his photos. He was a big bear of a man with a shiny bald spot on top and tufts of white hair on the side just above his ears. My five cousins reminded me too much of my brothers. They were tall and dark, with only a year separating them from the one who was next in line. Roberto was the oldest and closest to my age. We made the round of introductions, and then my cousins dropped on the couch or the floor, and I sat in a plush purple chair.

I was amazed at how comfortable I felt around them. My aunt bustled in and gave me an orange juice. Freshly squeezed juices are popular drinks in Italy.

"So what is your host family like?" Aunt Bianca asked in English.

"Wonderful," I told her. "Elena Pietra is an only child. It's a little strange. The house is very quiet."

"I know Elena," Roberto told me, also in English. "She is very nice."

"We hit it off," I assured him. "And I have my own room. At home I have to share my room with Maria." My younger sister by one year. A slob who always borrowed my clothes without asking.

Aunt Bianca wagged a pudgy finger at me. "You will miss your sister and all your brothers before the year is out."

"I seriously doubt it," I responded, but deep down inside, I had a feeling she was right. Although I had a habit of never revealing the good side of any of my siblings, I loved them beyond measure.

Uncle Vito glanced at his watch. "We must get to the restaurant. You can eat there, Carrina, if you do not mind eating alone."

"But don't expect fast service," Roberto announced. He shook his head. "Two of our servers are sick tonight, and we are always extremely busy."

Uncle Vito waved his hand. "My boys always help me in the kitchen. Tonight I will have to let one of them serve the customers, or food will go out cold."

I eased up in my chair. "I could wait tables for you," I offered. During my year in Rome, I had planned to come as close to having a vacation as possible, but they were family, after all. What would it hurt to work one night?

Aunt Bianca fluttered her fingers. "Don't be silly, Carrina. You are a visitor."

"I'm family," I pointed out. "Besides, I wait

tables in Dad's place, so I have the experience."

Uncle Vito looked uncomfortable. He moved both hands as though he were juggling invisible balls. Robin and Dana always teased me because I spoke with my hands constantly in motion. I'd always told them it was the Italian in me, and here I was discovering exactly how true that statement was.

"You see, Carrina," Uncle Vito said, "we have so many tourists that it's important we create an authentic Italian atmosphere."

"I'm Italian," I began. Then I realized that we'd been speaking in English from the moment I walked through the door. In perfect Italian, I said, "I speak Italian fluently. And I can speak English with an Italian accent."

Uncle Vito laughed. Aunt Bianca beamed. "Your papa, he taught you Italian?"

"Sì," I assured her.

Uncle Vito slapped his hands on his thighs. "Then tonight, you can work for us. We even have a uniform you can wear."

I stood up and smiled. *"Grazie."* I held up a hand, caught up in the moment. "But don't tell anyone I'm your American relative. Tonight I want to be a true Italian."

It was a role I'd never played before—but I could hardly wait.

TWO

Carrie

I'D FORGOTTEN EXACTLY how much I missed waiting on people—about as much as I missed raw, oozing blisters on my feet. And wearing a black pleated skirt, a stiff white starched shirt, and a black bow tie didn't increase my affection for the job. The uniform for Giovani's Pizzeria was a bit more laid-back—T-shirt and jeans.

Almost all the tables were occupied. Uncle Vito had introduced me to a few of the staff as the evening shift began, but many of his workers arrived a little later—with the crowds. All the workers spoke only in Italian—even to the customers.

Not only did tourists enjoy the restaurant, but so did a good many Italians. It was definitely to my advantage that I understood Italian. I wasn't exactly being a waitress. I was more of an all-around helper.

Clearing tables, getting second drink orders, putting fresh tablecloths on the tables, and setting out new silverware.

I glanced toward the front of the restaurant. Aunt Bianca looked calm as she explained to someone that it would most likely be a half-hour wait for a table. In Rome, evening meals usually didn't get seriously under way until around nine.

I glimpsed a dirty table and headed over. I stacked the plates, then the glasses, and lifted the whole thing. I hooked the rim of the top glass with my chin to prevent the tower of glasses from tumbling over.

I heard a couple of gasps as I passed some tables. I imagined I looked like a juggler in a circus. A balancing act on the verge of catastrophe. But I'd cleared too many tables for too long to think that I didn't know what I was doing.

Carefully I wended my way around the tables and headed for the kitchen. A swinging door kept the inner workings of the kitchen hidden from patrons. It occurred to me that tourists at least might enjoy watching the show that went on in the kitchen.

I pressed my shoulder to the door and swung it open. A guy with four plates running up one arm and a plate in his other hand jumped back.

"*Mi—Mi scusi,*" I stammered as I regained my balance and caught my breath.

"*Va bene,*" he replied in a deep, rich voice that reminded me of hot syrup dripping over pancakes.

I lifted my gaze from the plates he was expertly

balancing to his face—and lost my breath again as I stared into the most incredibly deep blue eyes that I'd ever seen. His eyes held me captive. The guy was tall, his blond hair combed back off his brow.

"Antonio!" Uncle Vito yelled. "Get the food out while it's hot."

Of course, Uncle Vito was yelling in Italian, but as usual, when it reached my brain cells, I heard in English.

Antonio gave me a charming smile, shrugged, and eased past me. I watched him stride through the restaurant with confidence. I appreciated the view of his broad back. And I liked the way his black trousers hugged his narrow hips.

With five brothers who constantly eyed girls and had no qualms about assessing their attributes out loud, I'd learned early on to pay as much attention to guys and not feel self-conscious about it.

And Antonio was definitely hot. I walked into the kitchen and deposited the dirty dishes near the sink. But I couldn't stop thinking about the guy I'd just seen.

Working here as a pinch waitress was going to pay off in ways I'd never imagined.

I hadn't come to Rome looking for romance, but when a romantic opportunity knocked—I wasn't foolish enough not to open the door.

Around eight-thirty I watched as Antonio began lining up empty tables. I really liked the way he moved—totally efficient. I could see the muscles rippling beneath his shirt. He wore a uniform like mine—almost. He wore black pants instead of a pleated skirt. But he had the starched white shirt and the black bow tie. I pictured him in a tuxedo, going to a prom—with me as his date, of course. That was a fantasy that would never come true. I wasn't even certain if they had proms in Italy.

My father had been more interested in discussing the Forum and the Pantheon than the social functions at the schools he'd attended. I assumed that was a typical male preference.

Aunt Bianca walked over to where Antonio was working. She began pushing the chairs against the tables he was arranging. "Carrina? Come here, dear," she said in Italian.

Okay, calm down, I ordered my heart. I was going to be able to get another close-up look at Antonio instead of watching him from afar—and hoping that no one noticed I was watching him.

"Yes, ma'am?" I said in perfect Italian.

She nodded toward the front, where a group of people had gathered. "Carrina, there are twenty people in this party. I want you to help Antonio serve them."

Help Antonio? Could I have asked for a better assignment? I wanted to hug Aunt Bianca. Throw my arms around her neck, kiss her cheeks, and promise her my firstborn child. Okay, I knew I was getting carried away, but this waiter was definitely the cutest of the bunch, and now I'd have a legitimate excuse to be near him. On the outside, I remained amazingly calm, while on the inside, I was doing a victory dance.

I shifted my gaze to Antonio. He was watching me speculatively. I felt myself grow hot under his perusal. "What do you want me do?" I asked in Italian.

He smiled warmly, shrugged, and responded in Italian, but of course, my automatic translate was working. "They are Americans, so they'll need menus. If you could get those—"

"Sure," I blurted out. "No problem." I'd already handed out menus to several Americans who had requested them. Few tourists understood that in Italy the waiters usually told patrons what foods could be ordered. Of course, waiters spoke in rapid Italian, and if a tourist wasn't familiar with the foods or the language, there was a good chance that the waiter was simply wasting his breath. Still, when in Rome . . .

"Then I'll take their orders," Antonio continued, "and you can help me bring out their food. Americans usually leave a tip. We'll split it evenly if this group does."

I knew that Italians weren't generally in the habit of tipping. My father had explained some of the social graces, although he'd been more concerned about teaching me how to keep my money out of the hands of pickpockets when I browsed through the open-air markets. My dad knew me

15

well enough to know that I wouldn't be able to re-sist the lure of the marketplace.

I grinned at Antonio. "Sounds fair." I jerked my thumb over my shoulder. "I'll get the menus."

"Carrina," he said softly.

I turned around to face him.

His gaze touched me like a caress. "A beautiful name," he murmured.

Then he strode toward the kitchen, leaving me standing there with a song of love humming through my veins. No one had ever told me my name was beautiful, and no one had ever spoken it with such a harmonious cadence.

I thought that I could definitely fall for this guy fast and hard.

I was accustomed to handling entire baseball and soccer teams at Giovani's Pizzeria. My dad's place was where all Little League sports teams as-sembled after beating each other—to create a show of good sportsmanship.

So helping Antonio with this group of Americans was a breeze. It was funny to watch the older girls giggle every time Antonio neared their table. It was so obvious that they'd developed crushes on him while he'd taken their orders. A couple of the guys at the table tried to flirt with me, but I pretty much nipped their amorous intentions in the bud when I told them that I had an older brother who wrestled bulls for fun. I whispered it in

English with an Italian accent so they couldn't mistake that I was *not* interested.

Antonio seemed to be enjoying the girls' attention, though. I guessed that I couldn't blame him. They were pretty much goggling at him like he was some movie star they'd spotted. I was surprised by how much it bothered me. I'd only just met the guy, and for all I knew, he could have a serious girlfriend. Guys this hot usually did.

We divided up the orders so we each made two trips, carrying five plates each. I could tell Antonio was a little impressed that I could carry four plates on my arm, one in the other hand—just as he did. My arms were tough. I was used to balancing pans of pizza and hauling pitchers of root beer.

All in all, Antonio and I made a good team. We didn't get in each other's way. I shadowed his moves. I let him lead. After all, he was the real employee here. And I simply followed, making sure everyone's order was perfect and everyone had a good time. It was actually a lot of fun. I thought of these people as my audience as I played to perfection the role of the Italian *cameriera*—waitress.

When they walked out of the trattoria, they left behind a tip that was the equivalent of forty American dollars.

"I can't believe this," Antonio said quietly as he handed me half the money. "I've never had anyone leave this much money."

"My papa always told me that great service equals

17

a great tip," I told him as I pocketed the money.

"Your papa," he repeated. "Lucky you."

Huh? What did he mean by that? He reached for a plate. We were still really busy, and I knew we didn't have time for idle chitchat. I'd have to pursue that avenue later.

"I'll clean the table," I offered. "You still have customers to serve, and I'm just a helper tonight."

"Thanks, Carrina."

I watched him head back toward the kitchen. I wondered why mentioning my pop seemed to bother him. Or maybe it was just my imagination. Maybe he was simply tuckered out. After all, we'd just worked together for an hour to keep this table of twenty—not to mention his other patrons—happy.

I was sure my dramatist imagination was going into overdrive because I too was a little worn out. Jet lag was beginning to take its toll. Only two days earlier I'd been in Texas, calling Dana and Robin to see what all they were packing.

I glanced at the table of dirty glasses, plates, and silverware. I groaned. Thank goodness, my waitress days were about to be behind me—at least until I returned to Mustang.

I looked toward the kitchen. Antonio came out, bearing an armload of plates loaded with spaghetti. Filling in tonight had definitely paid off. I'd met one hot and interesting guy.

Now I just needed to find out if he found me equally fascinating.

By the time the last customer walked out, it was close to eleven o'clock. And I had school tomorrow! But I wasn't tired. At home it was late afternoon. I was going to have to adjust to the time difference in a big way.

Aunt Bianca had tried to persuade me to leave when the crowd had begun thinning about half an hour ago, but I'd never left a job unfinished. My father had a really strong work ethic—an hour's work for an hour's pay. My brothers and I always rolled our eyes when he said it, but that didn't stop us from following his teachings.

Leaning over, I blew out the flame in the candle that adorned one of the tables. I loved the atmosphere that all the tall, flickering candles sitting in wine bottles had created. The wax dripped, flowing along the sides of the bottle until the wax hardened. I could see the drippings from so many other candles—a history of sorts. I wondered at all the people who might have sat here while the flame melted the wax.

I removed the tablecloth and wiped down the table, glancing casually over my shoulder to catch a glimpse of Antonio. Our paths had crossed several times after we'd waited on the group of twenty together. We hadn't had time to talk, but the more I saw him, the more he intrigued me. My heart sped

19

up every time we passed. He had the nicest smile and a way of making me feel like he was giving it to me as a special gift.

I couldn't explain it. He was so totally hot. I knew I was being shallow, judging the guy mostly by his looks and his ability to carry an armload of plates. But I had plans to expand my horizons where Antonio was concerned. Before I walked out the front door, I was determined to discover if he had a girlfriend. With five brothers who had way too many male friends, I wasn't exactly shy around guys. I'd learned early on how to hold my own.

I finished wiping the table. I leaned back, trying to work the kinks out of my lower back. My feet were swollen. Waiting on people was hard work. But the dining area looked clean now, so I figured my evening as staff at La Sera was about to come to an end.

I headed into the kitchen. And there was Antonio—and several of the other waiters—mopping the floor. Smiling, I pressed my shoulder to the wall and simply watched the way the muscles in Antonio's back and arms flexed beneath his shirt as he moved the mop over the floor.

"Americans," he spat, talking to the guy working next to him. "The girls, they are so stupid, so selfish. I hate waiting on them. They giggle like hyenas."

Stunned, I felt my mouth drop open. I couldn't believe what he'd said. What a loser! Had I actually spent most of the night drooling over this guy? He hated Americans. He thought we were stupid and selfish. Anger surged through me. As an American, I was neither stupid nor selfish.

Hadn't I sacrificed my evening to help out?

How small-minded to judge an entire group of people based on a few individuals. Boy, did I have a few choice words to toss at this guy. Hearing his comments had totally cooled any interest I had in him.

Hands balled into fists at my side, I took a step toward him—and halted.

Confronting him was way too easy. Telling him he was an idiot wasn't nearly enough. He needed to be taught a lesson he'd never forget. Someone needed to bring this arrogant Italian down a notch or two.

And I knew I was just the girl to do it.

Drama was my life back at Mustang High. So now I would have a larger stage—even if it was a smaller audience.

Antonio didn't know I was American. Why tell him I was?

I could get to know him a little better, give him the opportunity to get to know me. And when the time was right, when he was under my spell, I'd break the news to him that I was an American.

And gain retribution for all American girls everywhere!

Three

Antonio

I FELT THE hairs on the back of my neck prickle. Someone was staring at me. Hard. Intensely. A shiver traveled down my spine.

Or maybe I was just exhausted from a grueling night of waiting on people who had way too much money. Still, I looked over my shoulder.

And there was the new girl. Carrina.

Man, was she cute. And so exotic looking. She'd pulled her long, brown hair back in a ponytail, but I wanted to see it hanging loose around her face. And what a face. Her oval eyes were a dark brown—like expensive chocolate.

Tonight was the first time she had worked at La Sera, yet I had been amazed at the ease with which she had handled customers. Even the bratty Americans did not seem to bother her. I had seen her laugh with some of them as though they shared a private joke.

She fascinated me. And judging by the way she watched me, I thought that maybe I intrigued her. I wanted to get to know her better, but approaching girls was foreign to me. Ever since my papa had died, my life had narrowed down to work, school, and taking care of my sisters. Still, I did not want to let this opportunity to speak with her pass me by. Besides, I had a perfect excuse. She'd helped me out tonight. What would it hurt to thank her again? She wouldn't be able to read anything into that.

I took a deep breath to calm my nerves and repeated beneath my breath that girls were people too. Then I strode over to where she was standing near the wall.

I tried to give her a warm smile, but I had a feeling that my mouth probably looked like I'd just bitten into a lemon. Why couldn't I relax? After all, she was just a fellow worker. "I . . . I . . . uh . . . really appreciated all your help tonight." Now that I was really aware of her, it seemed that my tongue had forgotten how to form words.

She flashed a beautiful smile. "No problem."

Of course, it was no problem. She was paid to help. Now what should I say? Something clever would be good.

"I didn't catch your whole name," I confessed. Okay, not clever, but true. "I'm Antonio Donatello."

"Carrina Gio—Gio. Carrina Gio," she stammered.

Was she nervous as well? Briefly that made me feel better, but then I started to worry that maybe I was coming on too strong. I was most definitely nervous. I wiped my sweating palms on my trousers and tried to think of something else to say—something to fill the yawning abyss of silence stretching between us.

"Have you worked here long?" she asked.

I could have kissed her for that one. I was better at answering questions than asking them.

"Two years now." Two long years. Hard years. I did not want to think about them. I wanted to think about her. And I wanted to get to know her better. Much better.

"Listen, I know we just met, but . . . would you like to go have a cup of coffee at a nearby café?" I asked. I had a little extra spending money thanks to that generous tip the Americans had left. I held my breath.

Her mouth opened slightly. Her brow furrowed.

"I have a hard time unwinding after a hectic night," I explained quickly.

"Um . . . ," she began.

"The café is just around the corner," I assured her. "We can walk." I knew some girls were nervous about going places with guys they didn't know. Or maybe she had a boyfriend and was trying to decide whether or not he'd beat me up if she had coffee with me.

She nodded. "Yeah, sure. I would like to clean up a little first, though."

"Okay. It'll take me about twenty minutes to finish up here. I'll meet you out front," I told her.

She nodded quickly. I watched as she slipped through the swinging door, barely opening it.

I could only hope that she didn't have a boyfriend. Girls as cute as she was usually did.

I paced outside the restaurant. My nerves were a wreck.

Had I, Antonio Donatello, actually asked a girl out on a date?

No, no, this wasn't a date. We were just going to get something to drink and chat a little bit. Friends, maybe we would become friends.

I could certainly use one.

But a girlfriend? I had no time and very little money. It would be years before I could impress a girl enough to have a girlfriend.

The resentment rose up in me, and I shoved it back down.

Chill out, Antonio, I commanded myself. *There is nothing you can do about the past.*

And because of the past, it would be a long while before I could have the future I dreamed about. A future that included the one thing I wanted most: a girlfriend.

But what girl would settle for the little that I had to give right now?

The answer was obvious. No girl. Girls required time, attention, gifts, dates. . . .

The door to the restaurant opened. I watched Carrina step outside. Immediately I regretted asking her to join me. Usually I went to the café alone to unwind. Having someone with me tonight would only make it harder to go there alone tomorrow.

I was surprised to see Signora Romano hug Carrina. But then, Signora Romano had a tendency to treat everyone like one of her children. And Carrina was a new employee. I figured she just wanted to make sure Carrina felt good about her first night at work.

Carrina smiled brightly as she hurried down the steps. She wrapped her arm around mine. "Lead the way," she ordered.

Her flawless Italian carried an intriguing accent. I almost felt like it was a shadow over something else. I couldn't explain it. And I'd never known a girl to be so bold as to touch me like this. Especially after she'd seemed so hesitant to join me. Carrina was incredible. Totally relaxed, as though she were used to being around guys. Not a good sign. She probably had a bunch of boyfriends. I started walking toward the corner. "Tell me about your family," I prodded.

She groaned. "Boring. Five older obnoxious brothers, one younger spoiled sister." She looked up at me. "You?"

I smiled. "Four younger sisters."

She shuddered. "Italians always have such big families."

And the fact that she had so many brothers

might explain why she was so comfortable around me. Her brothers probably had lots of friends, and she was used to being around guys.

Unfortunately, except for my sisters, who were much younger than me, I was not used to being around girls. My heart was pounding. I was afraid she'd be able to hear it.

But if she did, she didn't say anything.

We rounded the corner. My mouth went dry when I saw the café. It was so plain. Suddenly I wished I'd offered to take her to a real restaurant.

"Is that it?" she asked, pointing toward the tables and chairs that lined the sidewalk in front of the café.

"Yes," I admitted.

"Awesome! I love eating at an outdoor café." She beamed at me.

"You do?" I asked.

"Truthfully, I've never eaten at one before, but I've always wanted to," she enthused.

I couldn't imagine how she'd avoided eating at a café. Maybe her family had to watch their money as carefully as mine did. Maybe they seldom ate out. For whatever reason, I was grateful for her enthusiasm.

I guided her toward a table away from the street. I wanted to be able to talk to her without having to shout over the roar of passing vehicles. Even though it was late at night, the streets were filled with people going places.

I ordered an espresso, and Carrina ordered a

caffè latte. I decided to splurge. I ordered us each a *tiramisú*. Her eyes brightened when she heard me order. I didn't very often spend money on myself. But then, neither did I ever find myself sitting at a table at a café with an exotic-looking girl.

She leaned forward and crossed her arms on the table. "I'll pay for mine."

I was seriously insulted. "I invited you. I'll pay."

She hesitated a moment before settling back in her chair. "Okay."

"Is working at La Sera your first job?" I asked. I wanted to know everything about her.

She looked slightly uncomfortable. "Uh, no. I worked at a pizzeria."

"Which one?" I asked.

She waved a hand in the air. "It was just a little one. You've probably never heard of it."

I nodded. "You're probably right. I don't eat out much."

"Do you like working at La Sera?" she inquired softly.

"I like working for the Romano family. They are good to me, fair to their workers," I admitted. "But I hate waiting on the rich Americans. They're such snobs."

She gave me a smile that seemed a little false. "I never noticed Americans were snobs."

"You probably haven't been around very many," I explained.

"Oh, I've been around quite a few," she assured me. "They seem nice to me."

"Nice?" I repeated. "Nice?" I raised my voice to a squeak. "'I want a vegetarian lasagna, but take out the peppers, and the onions, and the tomatoes.'" I returned my voice to normal. "How do you take tomatoes out of lasagna?"

She pressed a hand to her mouth, hiding a smile. A genuine smile this time. I knew because it touched her eyes.

"And then there's the pasta," I continued. "Americans call everything pasta. They don't understand that there's conchigliette, cappelletti, fusilli, farfalle, and a hundred others."

"Some understand," she protested.

"Not enough. An American couple orders cappelletti. I bring out the pasta that looks like little hats. The woman squeaks like she saw a mouse."

Carrina's smile broke free.

"You know this American woman?" I asked.

She shook her head.

"Be glad. Because like I said, she squeaks, 'Ah! Ah! That's not what I ordered!' Then she starts fluttering her hands, waving her arms like she wants to fly," I explained.

Carrina laughed. The sound was so lovely. I wanted to hear more, so I exaggerated the tale a bit.

"'I want butterflies,' she tells me. 'The pasta that looks like butterflies.' Then she gets out of her chair and starts floating around the room, dipping here, dipping there."

Shaking her head, Carrina laughed fully then, so

29

vibrant, so alive. Her eyes sparkled. "No, she didn't," she insisted.

"She did. You can ask Signora Romano. She disrupted everyone's meal. All because she wanted butterfly pasta."

The waitress brought over our pastry and drinks.

Carrina was still chuckling. "That's not being a snob," she argued. "That's simply trying to ensure that you get what you want."

"I have to take the pasta back and toss it in the garbage because she ordered the wrong thing. I have new pasta made—then her food is cold. All night I am going back to this one table, trying to please this one woman. My other customers get angry. Then no one is happy," I explained.

Carrina nodded slowly. I watched as she bit into her *tiramisú*.

"Maybe La Sera needs a place on the menu with photos of the actual pasta so the customers can point to what they want," she suggested.

I stared at her. "*We're* supposed to bend over backward because *they* are ignorant."

"They don't know they're ignorant. I don't think they mean to be trouble. They spent a lot of money to come here. They want authentic Italian cuisine—" She touched her fingers to her lips, kissed them, and then spread her fingers apart. "What's wrong with helping them have it?"

Pondering her question, I sat back and drank my espresso. I'd never considered the dining experience from an American's point of view. It troubled me to think she might have a valid point.

She leaned forward, moving aside her empty plate. "Enough talk about work. What do you do for fun?"

I lifted my cup—indicating I was doing what I did for fun—and gave her a half grin. "I'm a very exciting guy."

She laughed again, that remarkable laugh.

"I know you do more than drink coffee," she chastised.

"Let me see. For fun." My mind was an absolute blank. When was the last time I had fun? Right before my father was killed and I had to become the man of the family. "Honestly, Carrina, just sitting here talking with you has been more fun than I've had in a very long time."

"Then you definitely need a life," she stated, but not unkindly. Her eyes were sparkling as though we were sharing some inside joke.

I grinned. "I was thinking the same thing earlier this evening." And I was definitely thinking now that I wanted my life to include her.

Four

Carrie

ANTONIO DONATELLO WAS an arrogant Italian. I repeated the litany over and over as I sat at the breakfast table with my host family.

That he'd asked for my full name last night had caught me off guard and had me stammering like a novice actress. For all I knew, my aunt and uncle had mentioned to the staff that their American niece, Carrie Giovani, would be coming for a visit. Then when he'd asked me to join him at the café . . . ad-libbing, I'd quickly discovered, was not my forte. I was much more comfortable with script in hand. Still, once we'd gotten to the café, things had gone well—too well.

I didn't want to think about how much I'd enjoyed being with him. Or the way he'd made me laugh. Or the way he'd looked so deeply into my eyes that I felt he could see my soul. Heavy thoughts, but at the time they'd seemed so true. There was a sadness in his deep blue eyes. *From what?* I wondered.

Had he been feeding me a line when he said that talking to me was the most fun he'd had in a long time?

What if he hadn't been? It didn't matter. I couldn't let his words or his eyes distract me from my goal. I had gone out with him just to get even with him and his small-minded attitude toward Americans.

Granted, I could have told him at any time that I was born and bred in the United States. He'd given me plenty of opportunities—every time that he put down Americans. But I figured that the longer he thought I was Italian, the more stunned he would be when he learned the truth.

At least that was what I told myself. It was better than doubting my plan.

I found the silence at the Pietra table unnerving—I could actually hear myself think. I was accustomed to having meals with nine people talking at once, each louder than the other, fighting to be heard. Signore and Signora Pietra were very polite and reserved as they sat, drinking their coffee and eating a sweet roll. Italians usually had a light breakfast, unlike the plate of scrambled eggs, bacon, sausage, home fries, and toast that were heaped on my—and everyone else's—plate back home.

Their home was small, typical of Italians. Next to the tiny kitchen was the *tinello,* a medium-sized room where we ate our meals at a large table. Since

33

my arrival I'd spent most of my time in this room or my small bedroom. The house also had a *salotto*—which was the equivalent of a living room—but it was used only for formal entertaining. And occasional television watching.

"Nervous about your first day of school?" Elena asked, pushing a strand of silky, dark, short hair behind her ear.

Actually, until that moment I hadn't thought about it.

"A little," I confessed, now that it was on my mind. I would be attending the *liceo,* a secondary school that offered courses specializing in the languages, the arts, and the sciences. I planned to take at least one drama class. I was considering looking into a music class as well. Opera was big in Italy, and although it was considered a geek thing, I loved opera. Again, it was the Italian in my blood. Opera called out to me. "I can't believe your school days are so short," I admitted. School started at eight-thirty and ended at one-thirty. Everyone went home for lunch. No cafeteria food, no lunchrooms. A definite plus in my book since I never could figure out exactly what the food at school was made of.

Elena's pretty brown eyes twinkled. "The teachers give you enough assignments to keep you busy in the afternoons. And don't forget we have school on Saturdays too."

I groaned at that revolting thought. "A total bummer."

She laughed. "You Americans are spoiled."

Antonio had said the same thing, but it wasn't true. "Not really," I was quick to explain. "Our school days are longer. I think it all evens out."

"Did you enjoy meeting your relatives yesterday evening?" Signora Pietra asked me.

I smiled warmly at Elena's mother. "I loved meeting them. As a matter of fact, I'm going to be working in their restaurant for a while."

Signora Pietra furrowed her brow. "But I thought foreign-exchange students weren't supposed to work during their year abroad. Won't a job take away from traveling or having fun?"

"Maybe a little," I said. "But no matter what, family is family, and right now some of their staff is sick." Besides, the only way to see Antonio and finish teaching him a lesson was to work at the restaurant. It was the only place where our paths would cross. I couldn't very well just show up on his doorstep every day. I really wasn't looking forward to working regularly. After all, I had sort of envisioned this year as a vacation. Sure, I had school to attend, but that was nothing compared to my usual schedule at home.

But working would be worth it in the end. I couldn't wait to see the shock on Antonio's face when I finally told him the truth. Once he knew he'd misjudged Americans.

I was so excited as I walked the hallways of my new school. All around me I heard the rich cadence of

Italian. The school, housed in a white, one-story, meandering brick building, wasn't that different from my school back home. Students roamed the halls, talking, laughing, hanging out. Through the open doors I could see desks similar to the ones I sat in back at Mustang High. The only major difference was that the chalkboards were freestanding in many of the rooms.

I felt like the starship *Enterprise,* going where no Giovani had gone before. I was totally new at this school—the first Giovani in my family to grace its classrooms.

No teacher would say to me, *Miss Giovani, your brother Marcus was an ace at math. Why are you having problems figuring out the logarithm?*

No girl would try to be my best friend just so she could weasel a date with one of my older brothers. I'd learned early on to suspect any girl who complimented me or wanted to join me for lunch or acted like we were best buds when I didn't even know her name. Most were just striving to get information on my brothers.

Except Dana and Robin. My two best friends in the whole world. I treasured their friendship simply because they had absolutely no interest in my brothers. They cared about *me*.

Already I missed them. I'd spent a day with them in London before heading to Rome. I wanted to call them, but phone calls weren't cheap. We'd agreed to e-mail instead and if possible meet in a private chat room on the Internet. That would be fairly close to a phone call. Not as satisfying, to be sure, but better than nothing.

I'd checked my e-mail before heading to school. Carrie and Dana had sent me letters, explaining how nervous they were about their first day in a foreign school. I understood their nervousness. But I didn't share it. Sure, I was in uncharted territory—but I welcomed the adventure. The thrill of it all. I knew absolutely no one—and no one knew me.

Except Elena, of course. And a couple of my cousins who also went to school here. Like Roberto. Other than them, I wouldn't run into anyone I knew. It was a liberating thought. No one would judge me according to the low standards that my brothers had set.

I turned the corner and staggered to a stop. *No way!* the silent scream echoed in my head. I couldn't breathe. My heart hammered. A guy stood in front of a wall of lockers. Tall. Blond. I'd recognize him anywhere.

Antonio!

No, no, no. Not at *this* school. He couldn't be a student at *my* school!

But clearly he was. I watched him open a locker. He put something inside and slammed it shut with a metallic echoing. Then he turned in my direction.

Oh my gosh! I couldn't let him see me! I was supposed to be an American at this school. I couldn't be Italian as well!

Backing up, feeling my way along the hallway with my hand, I never took my eyes off him. A horrid thought flashed through my mind. What if we had a class together? He'd learn the truth way before I was ready for him to know. I'd have to reveal my true nationality because every teacher knew who the Year Abroad student was. How would I explain the situation to Antonio with people standing around us? What would his reaction be?

Maybe he wouldn't care. Yeah, right. After he'd put down Americans to my face? After I didn't tell him who I was? I felt pretty confident that he would care a great deal when he discovered I was an American.

Students kept weaving in and out between us, but soon it would just be him and me. Face-to-face. He was closing in on me. I had to escape and fast. I felt the smooth wood of a door. I jerked my head around. A bathroom. Great! A place to hide until he'd walked past. I pushed open the door and ducked quickly inside.

Realizing much too late that it was the boys' bathroom.

Five

Antonio

TODAY HAD BEEN the longest first day of school that I'd ever experienced. For the first time in a long time, I couldn't wait to get to work. Although it wasn't work that I was truly anxious for.

I was anxious for a glimpse of Carrina. So eager, in fact, that I arrived early at the trattoria. I opened the front door quietly and stepped inside. She was already there. Her back was to me as she stood at a table, filling salt-and-pepper shakers.

She was more elegant than I remembered. And so efficient as she filled the shakers, as though she'd done it for a lifetime. No one else was in sight. Quietly I tiptoed across the room until I was close enough to smell her perfume. A soft, flowery scent.

I leaned close to her ear. "Where have you been all my life?"

Carrina shrieked. She jerked back, her arms went up, and pepper rained over us. And when her arms came down, they hit the tray, and all the shakers took flight.

They showered the table, the floor, and us with salt and pepper.

Carrina sneezed. *"Achoo! Achoo! Achoo!"*

It was a cute sneeze. Small, tiny. She spun around. Her eyes were watering. She sneezed again. "What did you think you were doing?" she demanded.

I felt incredibly silly. I'd wanted to be romantic, and instead I'd been stupid and caused her to create a mess. I knew so little about girls, but I should have known I'd startle her. "I'm sorry." I bent down and began picking up the shakers. "I'll get these if you'll get the broom."

She knelt beside me and sneezed again. "I don't know where the broom is. I'll get these. You get the broom."

I hurried to the kitchen. Roberto raised an eyebrow at me. "What happened out there?" he asked. "I thought I heard Carrina scream." He was preparing the grill for tonight's crowd.

"I startled Carrina, but she's fine," I assured him as I opened the door to the closet and grabbed the broom and dustpan.

I rushed back into the main dining room. Carrina had picked up all the shakers. I watched as she tossed a pinch of salt over her shoulder.

"Superstitious?" I inquired as I neared.

She turned to look at me. Such deep brown eyes.

"You bet. You'd better take precautions as well," she advised. She held out the salt container.

Normally I was not superstitious, but right now I thought I could use some good luck with this girl. I wanted to get to know her so much better, and I didn't really know how to accomplish that goal. I extended my hand, and she poured a little salt into my palm. I tossed it over my shoulder. *Let her like me,* I wished silently.

I didn't even know if you were supposed to make a wish when you tossed salt over your shoulder, but I thought it couldn't hurt. Then I realized how selfish the wish was because I still had no more to offer her today than I had last night.

She took the dustpan and knelt on the floor. "I'll hold the dustpan; you sweep up the mess you made," she ordered.

"Me?" I scoffed. "I'm not the one who threw everything in the air."

She peered up at me. "You're not going to blame this on me."

I smiled. She was not easily intimidated. She no doubt was always arguing with her five brothers. Perhaps if my sisters were older instead of younger, I would know more about girls.

I swept up the grains of salt and flecks of pepper until the floor was spotless. Carrina stood and sneezed again. I took the dustpan from her. "You didn't answer my question."

41

She gave me a coy smile. "What question?"

"Where have you been?" I repeated.

Her smile blossomed. "Right here."

"But where? We don't go to the same school, or I would have seen you. Where is your family? Who are your friends?" I asked. I wanted to know everything.

She sighed and began refilling the shakers. "My two best friends are in the Year Abroad program this year. One is in London, the other in Paris."

"What a coincidence. My school is hosting a student in the Year Abroad program—an American." I started laughing. "I heard she went into the boys' bathroom today."

I expected Carrina to laugh. Instead her face turned red as though she were embarrassed. Was she shy about discussing bathrooms? I wanted to put her at ease.

I shook my head. "So typically American, to go to a foreign country where you don't know the language, to expect everyone to cater to you and put up signs in English. I hope my path crosses hers someday just so I can tell her how silly I think she is."

She looked like she might be ill. "Excuse me, will you? I need to get some more salt."

I watched her hurry into the kitchen as though she couldn't wait to get away from me. What had I done wrong?

Later in the evening, as I gathered the dirty dishes from one of the tables where I'd waited on patrons, I darted a quick glance around the dining room. No Carrina.

I had the distinct impression that Carrina was avoiding me. She somehow managed to be in the dining room when I was in the kitchen. In the kitchen when I was in the dining room. It was quite an elaborate little game of hide-and-seek. Sometimes she would even disappear for a while. Then I'd spot her talking with Signora Romano at the front. Tonight she was taking orders and serving customers. But she didn't seem as energetic as she did yesterday. Maybe she was simply nervous with the added responsibility.

The only other possibility was one I didn't like to acknowledge. I'd definitely done something to upset her. But what?

Carefully balancing the dishes, I crossed the dining room, pressed my shoulder against the swinging door, and shoved it open. Carrina stood on the other side—impressively balancing five plates on her forearm. We'd been like this when we'd first met last night—only in opposite places. She started to edge past me.

"I need to talk to you," I whispered.

"I'm busy." She averted her gaze.

"After work," I insisted.

She gave me a brisk nod, then marched into the dining room.

Never before had I felt so attracted to a girl. It was more than the beauty of her face. She worked hard. She had a nice laugh and a beautiful smile.

And there was something . . . different about her. I couldn't explain it, couldn't put my finger on it. But whatever it was, I liked it.

It was crazy for me to want to spend time with her based on absolutely nothing but a feeling. But I did. And in a few hours I would.

I went into the kitchen and deposited the dishes by the sink. We had two guys who washed all the dishes. I was glad that wasn't my job. I washed enough dishes at home.

Roberto was dipping a big ladle into a pot of steaming spaghetti sauce.

"What do you know about the new girl?" I asked him.

He stilled. "What?"

"Carrina. Do you know anything about her?"

Roberto looked me directly in the eye. "I know that my parents would *not* be happy if someone hurt her."

Wow! That was a heavy answer. Why would anyone hurt Carrina? I only wanted to get to know her, make her smile.

"Do you know if she has a boyfriend?" I prodded.

Roberto poured the thick sauce over the meatballs and noodles. "Look, Antonio . . ." His voice trailed off.

My heart sank. She did have a boyfriend. Last night she'd simply been nice. A friend. A fellow worker needing to unwind as much as I did. No wonder she was avoiding me. I had begun flirting with her the moment I came into the restaurant. I started to head back into the dining room.

"She doesn't," Roberto snapped as though he were seriously irritated with me.

I spun around and looked at him, hope sparking. "Doesn't what?"

"She doesn't have a boyfriend, but . . ." Again he seemed reluctant to continue.

"But what?" I prompted.

"But if you break her heart, my parents will kill you."

"Antonio!" Signore Romano yelled. "Don't you have customers?"

"*Sì!*" I shouted back.

Sì! Sì! Sì! She didn't have a boyfriend!

Carrina was sitting on the steps outside the trattoria by the time I finished helping close up. She stared at the vehicles whizzing by on the street. I wondered what she was thinking.

How did a guy figure out what a girl was thinking?

I dropped down beside her. She twitched as though I'd startled her again. She looked at me and smiled warmly. "No salt or pepper to spill this time," she said.

"I'm sorry that I startled you earlier," I admitted.

"No big deal," she assured me as she stood up, shoving her hands into the pockets of her pleated skirt.

"If you live near here, I thought I could walk you home," I suggested.

She smiled again. "Sure."

As we began walking, all I could think of was that I didn't get it. Had I done something wrong earlier today or not? Now she didn't seem to hate my guts. Granted, she wasn't exactly bursting with joy at the sight of me, but she had smiled at me twice. So why the cold shoulder all day? And why was she still being so quiet now?

I wished I'd spent more time with girls my own age. Yes, I'd had girlfriends; well, a few dates, a few weeks of dates, but the way girls' minds worked remained a mystery. The only girls I knew well were my sisters—and they still played with dolls. The silence stretching between Carrina and me was driving me crazy.

Every time we walked beneath a streetlight, I could see her face. Then the shadows moved in, and I could only guess at what she might be thinking. I figured the best approach was to just blurt out my concerns. "Did I say something to upset you?"

She glanced at me. I watched her nibble on her bottom lip as though she were trying to figure out exactly what she wanted to say. And in that moment I knew I'd blown it. I'd lost any chance of another date—if last night even counted as a date.

She sighed. "I've been thinking about that poor American student at your school. Trying to put myself in her place."

"Why would you want to do that?" I asked. She'd withdrawn from me because of the American?

Honestly, Americans were more trouble than they were worth.

"Because it helps me understand people if I try to imagine what it's like to walk in their shoes." She stared straight ahead, her expression serious. "So I'm seeing this girl walking through the halls of a school she's never been in before." She peered at me. "Do you remember how you felt the day you went to your school for the first time?"

Unfortunately, I did. I'd been terrified, petrified, afraid I wouldn't fit in. My friends had already dwindled down to just a few. Most didn't know what to say to me now that I had no father.

"I remember my first day at a new school," Carrina murmured, breaking into my thoughts. "I was excited but nervous. I knew only two or three people. I figure this Year Abroad student probably felt the same way, but I bet she was a little frightened as well. Even if she was unwilling to admit it to herself."

"Frightened?" I asked. *And who cares anyway?* I thought. *Why the big interest in the American?*

She held my gaze. "Frightened. She isn't sure what people expect of her. She's special. She has a role to play. She's representing her country, a country she loves, with a heritage she's proud of. Yet she's equally proud to be here, and she loves all that she's seen of Italy so far. But she has to project the image of the confident American. And maybe she's not quite as confident as she thought she would be. Maybe she worries about things. She studied

47

Italian. She can read Italian, but she gets nervous and goes into the boys' bathroom by mistake."

I raised my eyebrow. Whatever. I was much more interested in asking Carrina questions about herself than in talking about the scared American. Carrina's compassion was a surprise. That she cared so much about the silly foreign-exchange student was nice. Very nice. I don't think I'd be so silly as to go into the girls' bathroom if I were a Year Abroad student in the States, but . . . "Okay," I conceded. "Maybe that's what happened. Maybe she wasn't looking for signs written in English."

"Can you imagine how embarrassed she was?" Carrina prompted.

Okay, okay, enough already about the American! I was about to change the subject by asking Carrina why she felt such a kinship with the Year Abroad student, but she'd beat me to a question.

"What is your most embarrassing moment?" she asked softly.

I felt the heat burn my face. That I did not want to discuss with the girl I wanted to like me! "What does it matter?"

"Mine was walking into a boys' bathroom," she confessed. "Just like the American did today."

I stopped walking and stared at her. Ah. So that's why she felt so much sympathy for the girl.

She looked down as though she couldn't bear to meet my gaze. "It wasn't that long ago. I can re-member the moment vividly. Seeing those guys standing there when I'd expected to see girls putting on makeup. The worst part, the absolute worst part, was how quickly everyone heard about my faux pas. I could see people pointing, hear them laughing and snickering whenever I walked by. So I understand how your American student felt."

Idiot! I yelled at myself. I could kick myself in the shins so hard! *That is what you get for being so quick to judge people and for being so interested in your own ends, Antonio! You were so busy thinking about getting to know Carrina that you didn't even pay attention to her when she was trying to share something with you.*

I took her hand. "Carrina, I'm sorry. I didn't know. When I laughed about what the American did, when I said she was silly . . ." I sighed deeply, then realized that I was holding her hand. Worried that I'd been too forward, I pulled my hand away, supposedly to run it through my hair. No wonder Carrina had been upset with me. She must have felt like I was laughing at her when I'd joked about the American earlier. I had to undo the damage—no matter what the cost to my own stupid ego. "I told jokes with my fly open," I blurted out.

Now it was her turn to stop and stare at me. "Come again?"

"My most embarrassing moment," I admitted. I could still remember the sting of humiliation. "I was twelve. My friends and I approached a group of girls. I wanted to impress them, so I told a joke. They laughed. I told another joke. They laughed harder. Only later I discovered that they weren't laughing at my jokes. They were laughing because my jeans were unzipped."

She slapped her hand over her mouth, but still I heard a bubble of laughter trying to escape.

"You think it's funny?" I asked, trying to hide my smile. I was so relieved to see her laugh—to hear her laugh—and to see those brown eyes of hers sparkling again.

Carrina shook her head. Then she nodded and laughed. "Yes, I do." She held up a hand. "I'm sorry. But it is funny."

I smiled. "Maybe a little. And you know what? The American walking into the boys' bathroom is funny too. And when she goes back home to the States at the end of the year, it'll be the first story she shares with her family and friends, and she'll smile when she tells it."

"You really think so?" she asked, looking up at me thoughtfully.

"Definitely," I assured her, touched by how much she really did care about the girl. "In fact, if that were the kind of American that she was, perhaps I could like her," I admitted.

"Really?" she asked softly.

I nodded. "But Americans aren't like that. On second thought, she'll never think it's funny. I've worked at La Sera for two years. Americans—with their fancy clothes and their fancy cameras—complain, complain, complain. Nothing's funny to them. They don't know how to laugh at themselves. Hey, I have a great idea—why don't we forget Americans?"

She glanced at me, then stared straight ahead. "Most people are like that, Antonio. Not just Americans. I'll bet when you realized your zipper had been open while you were telling jokes to those girls, you didn't laugh about it right away."

She had me there. "Okay, maybe you're right."

She smiled. "Fine, so now that we're agreed on that, we can definitely stop talking about Americans."

We started walking again. I liked having her so close. I couldn't believe that I'd told her that embarrassing story about my zipper, but there was something about Carrina that made me feel I could tell her anything. I wanted to walk and walk and walk, ask her all about herself, where she lived, what she liked to do with her spare time. I wanted to know everything about this new girl who'd come into my life.

With a deep breath I slipped my hand back into hers. "Carrina, I want to be honest with you. Just tell you something outright."

She glanced up at me, clearly surprised.

"I really like you," I said, surprising even myself. "I've never felt this comfortable around a girl before."

Abruptly she stopped walking. She slid her hand out of mine. "Antonio, I . . . I . . . I'm sorry. I left something at the trattoria. I have to go back for it."

"I'll go with you," I offered.

She shook her head quickly. "No, please. I don't want to inconvenience you. Thank you for walking me this far."

I watched in stunned silence as she tore away and dashed up the street—never once looking back. Had I frightened her with my declaration? We only met yesterday. Had I moved too fast? I was being the only way I knew how to be. But perhaps that was not the way with Carrina? I thought girls liked guys to be strong and romantic.

Groaning, I started walking toward the bus stop where I would catch the bus home. I didn't understand girls. I didn't know what they wanted or what they expected.

All I knew was that I had opened up to Carrina, and it had meant nothing to her.

Six

Carrie

MY HEART POUNDED as I ran around the corner and headed back to the trattoria.

Antonio liked me. This very evening had been one of my dreams when I'd thought about living in Italy for a year. Walking down the beautiful, old streets of Rome, hand in hand with an Italian guy, soaking up the culture of my ancestors. But now . . . everything was a mess.

And the worst part was—I liked him. I hadn't expected that. He had such a warped view of Americans, but somehow I understood his position a little better than I had when I'd first heard him put down the people of my country. As someone who worked in a restaurant that catered to tourists, what he knew of Americans was limited to what he saw of Americans: the ones who visited the trattoria and complained, making his job even harder than it was already.

But instead of telling him that he was wrong, that not all Americans were like that, that I, in fact, was American and if he'd get to know me, he'd see how wrong he was, I had decided to play a game.

Not a role. A *game*. Like I was in middle school. Like I was a child.

How in the world was he going to feel when he discovered I was an American? And not just any American? *The* American.

Suddenly I felt mean and spiteful.

I'd deliberately started our walk in a direction that wouldn't lead to my home. So I could add deceptive to the list of my awful traits. But I couldn't risk letting him know where I lived. What if he knew Elena? What if he knew Elena was hosting his school's Year Abroad student? I'd been surprised enough today to realize that my aunt, uncle, and cousins hadn't mentioned my background to the staff of La Sera. I knew they wanted to project the image that only native Italians worked there, so perhaps the Romanos hadn't shared my nationality with their employees just to make sure the secret didn't leak.

What if Antonio realized that the YA student was me?

I'd known at some point—as we walked in the wrong direction—that I was either going to have to blurt out the truth about myself or find an excuse to leave him standing there. Once he'd told me he liked me, blurting out the truth was no longer an option.

I'd wanted to teach him a lesson. I hadn't wanted to hurt him! And telling him the truth would only make it seem like I'd been making a fool out of him.

I arrived at the trattoria and found Elena's scooter where I'd locked it up earlier. Slipping the helmet on my head, I straddled the scooter, then turned the ignition and rolled onto the street. The scooter sounded like an angry bee buzzing around me.

Oh, how I longed for the quiet of Mustang so I could think. Sure, it was noisy at home, but I could always go to Robin's farmhouse for quiet since she was an only child and lived outside of town. I needed to talk to my friends—desperately.

What would they think? Would they think I was cruel?

This farce had gone on long enough. I needed to end it—and soon!

But how? How could I end it without causing him to hate me?

When I arrived at the Pietras, my host parents were just finishing a cup of tea. After I'd assured the signora that I didn't want a single thing, she and her husband kissed me good night and went into their bedroom. Elena must have been sleeping already. I rushed up to my bedroom, grateful for the solitude.

My room was tiny, but I loved it. The bed had a brass-railing headboard, which I thought was incredibly romantic. The small wooden desk held my laptop computer and a telephone, and beside the desk was a white miniature dresser with gold paint etched along the edges. It looked ancient—like everything in Rome. And I adored it.

I sat on the edge of my bed and stared at the phone. Who should I call? Dana? She was Miss Practical. She would *not* understand what I'd done or why I'd done it—but she would have a reasonable solution to my dilemma. She looked at everything with the broad strokes of an artist.

Or maybe I should call Robin. Dare-me-to-do-anything Robin would certainly understand my need to trick Antonio. She would also approve. Be Daring was her motto; well, at least until she'd arrived in London and decided she was going to change her personality from outgoing to demure. Robin thought the English wouldn't approve of her unless she acted—and even spoke—differently. In a way, Robin was being her usual daring self by pretending to be quiet. I just hoped she reverted back to her great self once she realized that people would like her just as she was, no matter what country she was in.

After all, I was a perfect example of what could happen when you pretended—no matter what the reason—to be someone you weren't.

I needed both my friends for advice. But I couldn't afford to call both of them. Heck fire, I couldn't afford to call one of them. I crossed my small room and opened the double doors that led onto the balcony. I wrapped my fingers around the black wrought-iron railing. I felt like Juliet from *Romeo and Juliet*, like a star-crossed lover.

Rome. Roma. Romance. It was a city meant for romance, and I'd unexpectedly fallen under its spell. No tall office buildings or skyscrapers marred the skyline. It looked as it had for centuries, with Corinthian columns and the cupolas of baroque churches silhouetted against the sky. The view was breathtaking. And it made me feel insignificant and wondrous at the same time. I couldn't explain it.

Although my balcony was bare, I could smell the flowers from all the other balconies. When a city had three million people, it didn't leave a lot of room around houses for gardens, so many people had created little gardens with pots and pots of beautiful flowers and lush plants.

My head throbbed. I rubbed my temples. Antonio liked me. Isn't that what I'd wanted? Snare him. Get him to like me and then, with the perfect smirk, announce: *But how can you possibly like me? I'm an American.*

The words had been on the tip of my tongue. . . . If only he hadn't been so apologetic when I told him that I'd walked into a boys' bathroom. He didn't know I'd been talking about that very morning, but I had described to him exactly how I'd felt when I'd seen guys standing in the white-tiled room. It had been without a doubt the single most embarrassing moment of my life.

A couple of the guys had laughed. The other four had simply stared at me with mouths agape. And I'd stared back before dashing out, my hair covering my face, just in case Antonio had been there. So I'd waited until the guys cleared out and the bell rang. I'd been late to my first class. By the time I got to my last class, the rumors had circulated throughout the school. The female Year Abroad student had gone into the boys' bathroom. I heard them whispering about it and giggling. They didn't seem to be laughing at me in a mean-spirited way, but that hadn't made me feel any better.

Yet I knew someday I *would* laugh about it. Just like Antonio said I would. Certainly the story would have my brothers rolling on the floor. That thought made me smile.

"Carrie?" a soft voice whispered.

I turned to see my host sister, standing in the doorway of the balcony. "Hi, Elena. I thought you'd already gone to bed."

"No, I was reading a magazine," she said in English. "Are you all right?" She stepped onto the balcony. Elena had told me she wanted to speak English with me as much as possible in order to practice. She spoke English almost as well as I spoke Italian.

I sighed. I was far from okay, but I didn't want to worry Elena. "Just thinking."

"I heard that your first day did not go as smoothly as you'd hoped," she murmured.

I looked at the black sky. "Nothing is going as I'd hoped."

"Everything will be okay, Carrie," she consoled me. "Just give it some time."

I turned around and smiled at her. "I know you're right. It's just hard right now, I guess." I felt guilty.

We were talking about two different things, but I so appreciated the kind words, even if she thought I was referring to the infamous Bathroom Episode.

"How did you manage to go into the boys' bathroom?" she asked, clearly baffled. "You can speak and read Italian better than some Italians I know."

I sighed again. "It's a long story." I crossed my arms over my chest and leaned back against the railing. "Do you happen to know Antonio Donatello?"

"Sure, I know him," Elena said. "He works at La Sera. But since I don't work there, I don't know him too well."

"Don't you know him from school?" I asked.

"Not really," Elena replied. "Antonio doesn't have a lot of time for hanging out or after-school events."

"Why?" I asked. Probably because he worked at La Sera. A part-time job didn't allow for much socializing or school activities.

"Because his papa died," Elena explained. "He has to be so responsible for his family."

I gasped and felt my heart tighten. I remembered how quiet he'd gotten our first night at the café when I'd mentioned my father. Had it made him think of his own father? "His papa died? How?"

"An automobile accident," Elena said solemnly. "A drunk driver." She shook her head. "It's such a sad thing. Antonio is the oldest, the only boy. When his mama works, he takes care of his four younger sisters. When his mama isn't working, he is."

"Oh gosh." I pressed my arms against my chest,

trying to ease the ache I felt. Poor Antonio. "When did his papa die?"

"Two years ago," Elena told me.

Two years. That was exactly how long Antonio had been working at La Sera. In light of this new information, my ploy to teach him a lesson seemed incredibly petty now. What had he really done? Taken a dislike to Americans because they were rude and impatient and mean when they came into the restaurant.

Wouldn't he dislike them a whole lot more when he found out that I was an American and had been taking him for a ride?

Stupid plan, Giovani, I chastised myself. I had to tell Antonio the truth right away.

And suffer the humiliation and the consequences that would follow.

The next day at school I felt like I was constantly playing dodgeball—only I was playing dodge Antonio. I peered around every corner, scoped out every hallway. I'd gone from boldly going where no Giovani had gone before to *sneaking* where no Giovani had sneaked before.

If my new classmates thought me strange yesterday, they must have found me downright bizarre today. I was grateful when the school day ended, as it always did, at one-thirty. Since all the kids went home for lunch with their families, I didn't have to worry about a cafeteria confrontation—with my classmates about how weird I was . . . or with Antonio.

After my last class I decided to drop by the school library. In my history class we'd been assigned a research paper on a famous artist. We were studying the various churches in Rome, and they all had some amazing artwork. I'd chosen to write my paper on Michelangelo.

As I wandered down the aisles between bookshelves, it was a kick to see all the books with Italian titles—books I'd read in English. The classics, like *Tom Sawyer* and *Charlotte's Web* and *Hamlet,* plus the ones Robin, Dana, and I traded, like the Harry Potter books.

Suddenly my heart stopped. I heard Antonio's voice—asking for the biography section. He had to be standing at the front desk. I heard the librarian's voice but not her response. Footsteps echoed over the wooden floor. Nearer, nearer. Panic hit me.

I ducked around the corner. Straight into a dead end. Bookshelves on either side of me but no exit—except the opening through which I'd come. This was almost as bad as ducking into the boys' bathroom. Would I never learn to look before I ducked?

The footsteps came closer, closer. My heart pounding, I grabbed a book, opened it up, and held it in front of my face.

The footsteps stopped. I barely breathed. *Dare I lower the book?* I wondered.

"Have you seen any other biographies on Raphael?" Antonio asked.

I nearly jumped out of my skin. What was he talking about? I peered at the chapter opening I had the book open to: "Raphael's Early Works." Oh.

I'd grabbed a book on the very artist he was researching! "No," I replied in a falsetto voice.

"Excuse me," he said. "I need to get to those books on the other side of you."

I pressed my back to the shelf while he edged past me. Out of the corner of my eye I could see him crouching, searching the books. He pulled a book off the shelf and riffled the pages.

"I have to do a research paper on an artist for my history class," he said conversationally. "But it looks like you've got the only book on Raphael. Guess I'll do it on Botticelli." All the junior-year history classes must have the same assignment, I realized.

I brought the book closer to my face as he stood up.

"Raphael is one of my favorite artists," Antonio added. "Don't suppose you want to do your report on Botticelli?"

"No," I whispered. "Sorry."

"I didn't think so, but it never hurts to ask." Unfortunately, I heard the disappointment in his voice.

I listened to his footsteps echo as he walked away. Fainter, fainter. I pressed the book against my face. A close call. Too close.

Because of me, because of my stupid plan and my stupid need to hide from him until I could bear to tell him the truth, Antonio couldn't do his paper on Raphael. How could the library have only one biography of Raphael? With his work schedule Antonio probably didn't have much access to the Internet to do school research. Sneaking in some reading during breaks and before bed was probably his only time to study.

When I heard him leave the library, I grabbed a book on Michelangelo and strode to the counter, the Raphael biography still in hand. The librarian smiled at me. "How do you like going to school in Rome?" she asked.

"It's definitely not like attending school in the States," I told her. In Mustang, I walked the halls like I owned them. I'd pretty much planned to do the same thing here. Instead I was creeping through the hallways like Sidney in *Scream,* waiting for the guy wearing the distorted white mask to jump out at her. "But I sure do like it here," I added, placing the biography of Michelangelo on the counter. "Especially getting out so early."

She smiled as she stamped the book for me. "Ah, but you Americans are not used to school on Saturdays."

"I will be after this year," I told her with a smile. "Could you do me a favor?"

"Sì," she told me. "If I can."

I slid the book on Raphael toward her. "The guy who was just in here—"

"Antonio Donatello?"

I nodded. "He was looking for a book on Raphael but couldn't find it. I found this after he left. It was shelved in the wrong place," I whispered as though I intended to keep this horrible alphabetical offense between us. "Could you send a note to him in class tomorrow and let him know that this book is available?"

She smiled and took the book. "Yes, I'll do that."

I leaned forward. "Don't tell him that I found it. I'm sure some student put it back on the shelf carelessly."

She gave me an appreciative smile. "I'm used to that."

I took the Michelangelo biography, shoved it into my backpack, and walked out of the library. At least now Antonio could do his report on Raphael. I felt a little better knowing that, but not much.

After all, I'd let the perfect opportunity to reveal myself pass me by. All right, I'd let it pass me by because it was not so perfect. That wasn't quite the truth either. It wasn't quite the perfect spot for me. I wanted to tell Antonio the truth, but preferably someplace with no witnesses. I figured his home turf would be best. And chicken that I was, I was thinking about waiting until Saturday to talk to him so we'd have Sunday—a whole day without our paths crossing—to lick our wounds.

Besides, I needed to figure out the best way to announce my deception. Every line that I ran through my head sounded like it came from a bad play. Perhaps I had better just tell him the truth in as straightforward a way possible. I supposed I could start with my name. Carrina Gio. That was what he thought my name was!

Antonio wasn't a slouch in the intelligence department. I knew it was only a matter of time before he realized how close Carrina Gio and Carrie Giovani were. What had I been thinking when I'd come up with that lameoid variation of my name?

Obviously I hadn't been thinking. My emotions had been dictating my actions. And my emotions apparently weren't real bright.

I'd never in my life been so angry with myself. Because the truth was, I liked Antonio. I liked him a lot. He was an interesting guy, complex. He'd been honest and open with his feelings, whether about Americans or me, a girl he thought he liked and wanted to know. When he wasn't putting down Americans, he was easy to talk with. And he was so totally hot to look at.

When I got home from school, I called Aunt Bianca to ask if she needed me at the trattoria. Score! The guys who'd been sick were now fine, so I wasn't needed for the rest of the week! I told Aunt Bianca that was great news since I had so much schoolwork to do that I would have trouble working and keeping up with my studies. In fact, I added, if anyone at La Sera asked why I wasn't working, she could just tell them that I was taking the week off to work on my school projects. That way, I knew, Antonio wouldn't think my sudden absence had anything to do with him, and he wouldn't ask questions that might reveal who I really was.

That settled, I logged on to the Internet. First I typed Antonio's name into a search engine and prayed. Bingo! There he was. His name and address. He didn't live very far from La Sera. I copied the address, then entered the private chat room that Carrie, Dana, and I had learned how to access.

We'd agreed to meet at a certain time every few days to chat, vent, get advice, and feel like we were together. Yesterday I'd told them a little about Antonio. Dana had told us that Alex Turner Johnson, a guy from Mustang, was in Paris and most of her classes. She was annoyed because she was attracted to him, a regular guy from home, when her dream was to find a French boyfriend.

Robin had discovered that her gorgeous host brother, Kit, had a girlfriend. A total bummer. She had a major crush on the guy, and I couldn't blame her. She was still hiding her real personality.

Our year abroad was off to a bad start for each of us. We all needed each other more than ever—and we were in different countries.

Carrie: *Hey, guys. How's it going?*

Dana: *Other than the fact that I can't seem to escape Alex Turner Johnson—it's going great. Why does he have to be so cute when I only want to be attracted to hot French guys?!*

Robin: *It's hard living with a guy when you really like him—especially when he treats you like a sister! I wish he didn't have a girlfriend.*

Carrie: *Looks like we have guy troubles all the way around.*

Dana: *What's happening with Antonio?*

Carrie: *I have to tell him the truth. That I'm an American. I'm just not sure how to do it.*

Dana: *Uh, Antonio, I'm really sorry I didn't tell you this before, but, um, I'm an American. No, not just*

an American. *The American you made fun of for*
walking into the guys' bathroom. The American
you assumed was silly and stupid.

Robin: *Yeah, but guess what? I'm not after all! See,*
Americans are great! Um, you forgive me for
lying to your face, right?

Carrie: *Come on, I need real help here! I can't just say all*
that. Can I? What am I going to say?

Robin: *Did you ever actually tell him that you were Italian?*

Carrie: *No, I just did my best to make sure he assumed I was.*

Dana: *What's the worst thing that could happen when he*
learns the truth?

Carrie: *He could hate me.*

Robin: *So you like him.*

Carrie: *Way too much.*

By the end of the week I was a wreck. I'd spent
most of my time at school hiding out in the girls'
bathroom . . . which really limited your social life
and the "Italian experience." So far, most of my
conversations had revolved around makeup, hair-
styles, fast food, and television shows—not that I
minded discussing any of those topics. But there
quickly came a point where you'd said all you cared
to about eye shadow, McDonald's, and *Felicity*. And
I'd also done absolutely no sight-seeing. My parents
had asked for details about Rome's architecture and
ruins and street life, and I'd been embarrassed to report back that I hadn't had time to do any sight-
seeing yet. I'd been so obsessed with the stupid lie

between Antonio and me that I'd gone straight from school to the Pietras'. I'd spent a lot of time on the balcony outside my bedroom.

There was no way I could complain, however, about my limited social life or sight-seeing schedule. After all, Antonio's very existence was limited and for a very sad reason. Whenever I saw him in the hallways, he was alone. Always alone. He didn't hang around in cliques. I didn't see him laughing hysterically with guys. I didn't see him lounging against his locker, looking the girls over as they walked by—which a lot of the guys did do.

Between school, work, and caring for his sisters, he obviously had no time for friends; he'd probably lost the ones he used to have. The guys at La Sera were probably the only acquaintances he had.

He'd reached out to me—not knowing that I planned to betray his friendship.

I felt like a complete and absolute jerk.

When Saturday arrived, I absolutely could not bring myself to go to school one more day. I couldn't play dodge Antonio one more minute. I couldn't risk our paths crossing before I'd told him the truth. I explained to Signora Pietra that I wasn't feeling well, which was true. Then I sat on my balcony, running words through my head, trying to come up with a way to explain to Antonio why I, Carrie Giovani, wasn't exactly as he thought Americans were— selfish and spoiled, only interested in myself.

Seven

Antonio

I STOOD IN the tiny kitchen and glared at the slab of butter that was slowly melting in the pan.

My mama was at work. My sisters were playing in their rooms. And I was fixing lunch. Typical Saturday afternoon routine. Dull, boring. Not at all the way that I'd planned to spend my teenage years.

I had never resented that my papa died in an auto accident—until now. Certainly I had despised the driver who had gotten behind the wheel of a car after drinking too much wine—but I'd never blamed my papa.

But suddenly I was tired. Tired of being the oldest. Tired of working. Tired of going to school. Tired of being alone.

Sure, I had family, but family wasn't a girlfriend. And I wanted a girl in my life. A girl like Carrina.

I had tried to stay angry with her after she had run off. But if I was honest with myself, I couldn't blame her. We hadn't spent enough time together to really know each other. Yet I'd announced that I liked her and expected her to respond with equal fervor.

Stupid, Antonio, I berated myself. *Stupid. You have to take a girl out, treat her special, show her that you care.*

Not announce it like an advertisement.

But dating was out of the question. My mama needed every lira that I could hand over each night. Even if she didn't, where would I find the time? Perhaps it was best that I'd ruined my chance with Carrina. She simply wasn't interested. She'd been so eager to avoid me that she'd even taken the week off from work; Roberto had mentioned that she needed some extra time to study. I was sure she simply needed extra time away from me. From me and my stupid mouth.

I tossed diced onions and peppers into the skillet and listened to them sizzle. The gray smoke rose.

No, I'd never blamed my papa. But then, never before had I craved some time that was mine alone, time that wasn't taken up with school, work, or watching over my sisters.

If only Carrina did like me back. I'd find a way, find the time, to take her on a real date or just a walk home after work. I'd show her how much I truly wanted to get to know her. And maybe she'd see that I wasn't just being a romantic type when I'd told her how comfortable I felt with her. When I was with

Carrina, whether watching her those two days at La Sera or walking her that short distance from the trattoria, I felt like my troubles didn't exist anymore.

I heard the doorbell ring. Who could that be? Probably one of my sisters' friends. I really wasn't in the mood to have a bunch of laughing, giggling, talking girls in the house. But I wanted my sisters to be happy. Even if I wasn't. So I'd quietly suffer through the invasion of their friends.

I wiped my hands on the flowery apron I wore. My mom's apron. She liked bright colors and flowers and combined the two whenever possible. The doorbell chimed again. I jerked it open, prepared to be run over by five giggling preteens.

But the girl of my dreams stood before me, staring at my apron, her lips twitching as though she was fighting not to laugh.

I felt the heat of embarrassment burn my face. I jerked off the apron and balled it up. I was mortified that I had been caught wearing it, but the longer I kept my jeans clean, the less laundry I had to do.

"What are you doing here?" I asked. I was stunned. How did she know where I lived? Why was she here? I'd thought I totally turned her off.

Carrina bit her lower lip and stared at the ground. "I just wanted to talk to you."

I studied her. Now that I was looking at her, I could still feel the sting of her rejection the night I started walking her home. Was she here to tell me she wanted me to leave her alone at work?

"You didn't seem so anxious to talk to me the other night," I reminded her.

She blushed. A pretty blush. I wished that I hadn't noticed. I wished I could stay irritated with her. But I was really incredibly glad to see her—after what seemed like an eternity since we'd last talked.

She held up her right hand, and I saw a pewter ring on her finger. "I'd left my ring at the trattoria that night—it's what I'd had to go back for."

She took it off and shook it. It broke apart into several thinner rings, all dangling from one main ring. "This is a puzzle ring," she explained. "It took me forever to figure out how to put it together when it came apart. I didn't want to risk it disappearing and having to get another one. Each ring goes together differently."

I watched as she put it back together. She had such delicate hands. She slid the ring onto her finger and looked at me expectantly.

"You haven't been at work this week," I pointed out. "Roberto said you had a lot of school-work to do and wouldn't be keeping a regular schedule at La Sera."

She scuffed the toe of her sneaker into the ground. "Yes, um, I did have a lot of school projects this past week."

I leaned against the doorjamb, drinking in the sight of her. I couldn't believe how glad I was to see her. But I definitely could not invite her into the house. I didn't want her to see the mess. My sisters had been little terrors this morning, and the house looked it.

"What did you want to talk about?" I prodded.

She stood on her tiptoes and looked over my shoulder. I shifted to block her view of dolls, puzzle pieces, and crayons.

She furrowed her delicate brow. "Is something burning?"

I cursed under my breath. My onions and peppers!

I rushed into the kitchen and groaned at the sight of black smoke spiraling toward the ceiling. Too late!

I turned off the stove and lifted the pan. I glared at the charred remains that were now burned to the bottom of the pan. I'd used the last of the onion and pepper. So now my sisters would complain because the spaghetti sauce I'd planned to feed them for lunch would be bland. I could hear them now.

"Blah!"

"Antonio, what's wrong with this?"

"Don't you know how to make spaghetti sauce?"

"Why don't you get a girlfriend who can come over and cook for us?"

My sisters were always harping that I needed to get a girlfriend. I don't know why they cared.

I dropped the pan into the sink, turned on the water, and heard the hiss as it hit the hot pan. I'd have to scrub it. I tossed the apron I'd balled up earlier onto the counter. Then I remembered why I'd taken it off.

I glanced over my shoulder. Carrina stood in the kitchen, watching me. "Lunch," I announced dejectedly.

I heard pounding footsteps. My sisters skidded

into the kitchen, barely missing Carrina.

"What's that stink?" Gabriella asked. She was six. Her crayons littered the living room.

"Did you burn lunch again?" Isabella asked. She was eight. Her dolls were strewn over the living room.

"I'm gonna tell Mama," Luisa announced. She was ten. She dropped puzzle pieces everywhere, so her hundred-piece puzzles were never finished.

"I'm hungry," Mara whined. She was twelve and hinted more than the others that I needed a girlfriend—someone who could show her how to apply makeup.

"Who are you?" Gabriella asked. She was staring up at Carrina.

Carrina smiled warmly. "I'm Carrina."

"Are you Antonio's girlfriend?" Luisa asked.

"No, she is not my girlfriend," I stated quickly.

"Antonio's never had a girlfriend before," Mara announced.

"Out!" I shouted. I didn't need my sisters to reveal the whole history of my dull and boring life. I waved my arms in the air. "Get out!"

"But I'm hungry," Isabella cried.

"Then get out so I can fix lunch. Go!" I yelled.

They turned to leave. Luisa giggled. "He just wants us to leave so he can kiss her," I heard her say as they walked out of the kitchen. I wanted the floor to crack open and swallow me. Where was an earthquake when I needed one? Or a volcanic eruption? Pompeii had been obliterated. Why not me?

I gave Carrina an apologetic shrug. "I'm sorry.

Right now is not a good time. I have to fix lunch for my sisters and finish cleaning."

A bubble of laughter erupted from her throat. It was such a pretty sound even if she was laughing at me.

"What?" I demanded.

She pointed toward the arched doorway where my sisters had shuffled out. "They remind me so much of my brothers. If a guy stopped by the house to borrow a schoolbook, my brothers would give him and me a hard time—make kissing sounds. Guys learned real quick to avoid my house or suffer the consequences."

I smiled and leaned against the counter. "Really. So only a brave guy would date you."

She laughed as though completely comfortable with herself. "Right. And most don't stay brave for long."

"I would." I glanced at the murky water in the pan. I hadn't meant to admit that. I realized that I would face her brothers for an opportunity to go out with her—but even that wasn't enough for us because I still didn't have time, and I didn't have money.

I turned my attention back to her. "I've got to fix lunch. What was it you needed to tell me?"

"Uh . . . it can wait." She pointed her thumb over her shoulder. "I noticed a pizzeria around the corner on my way here. Why don't I treat you and your sisters to some pizza?"

"No way. Girls don't pay—"

"They do when they're responsible for you burning your lunch," she explained.

"No," I declared adamantly. I really wanted to

spend time with her and wondered if the money in my pocket would cover a pizza.

She took a step closer. "Antonio, it's my fault your lunch is ruined. Please let me take you and your sisters out. Otherwise I'll feel guilty for the rest of my life." She pressed the back of her hand to her forehead and looked up at the ceiling. "Forever, it will eat at me," she crooned dramatically. "The guilt, the guilt will destroy my dreams. I'll have no chance for happiness—"

I laughed at her dramatic display. "All right," I conceded. "But I don't think you truly understand what you're getting yourself into—hauling my four sisters around."

"It can't be any worse than traipsing after five brothers," she assured me.

Carrina was amazing. I could not believe the way she handled my sisters. Or should I say the way she *bribed* them. If they wanted pizza, they had to help clean the house. I'd never seen my sisters so enthusiastic about cleaning. No whining. No pouting. They were willing to do whatever Carrina asked because she promised them a reward.

She even helped me clean the kitchen.

I was putting away the ingredients that I'd taken out earlier for my sauce when I heard Carrina shout, *"En garde!"*

I turned around. She was brandishing a celery stick. She tossed one at me. She held hers out and placed her

76

other hand on her hip. "Defend your right to clean the charred remains from the pan," she ordered.

Dumbfounded, I stared at her. What was she doing?

She bounced toward me, waving the celery stick in the air.

"Fight, Antonio!" She slapped her celery stick against mine.

I couldn't believe she wanted to have a fencing match in the kitchen using celery sticks as rapiers.

With the flowery end of the celery she poked my chest. "Defend yourself!" she commanded.

"Carrina," I began.

She tilted her head at me and smiled, then hit my celery stick. This was crazy. Totally insane! I, always amazingly calm, straight-as-an-arrow Antonio, struck back. Her eyes widened before she pounced again.

The next thing I knew we were thrusting and volleying and darting around the kitchen. Feinting here, striking there. I'd never done anything so . . . incredibly childish.

Or had so much fun!

Carrina was laughing, her wondrous laugh. But even so, she never lost sight of her goal. To beat me. Our celery sticks clashed high, met low.

Suddenly she struck mine, and it went sailing across the kitchen.

"I won!" she shouted. She tossed her celery stick to me. "I'll clean the pan."

"But it's a mess," I pointed out.

She raised an eyebrow. "Then you should have

fought harder to defend your right to wash it."

I watched as she rolled up her sleeves and attacked the pan with the same enthusiasm that she'd had when she attacked me with a celery stick. The winner shouldn't have to wash the pan. The loser should have to, but I didn't want to argue with her. I just wanted to enjoy her presence.

I wiped down the counters while she scrubbed the burned onions and peppers out of the pan and made it shine. Then she dried it. When she was done, she flicked my backside with the towel. "Come on, Antonio, work faster!" she urged.

"Come on, Antonio," my sisters cried from the living room. "Work faster!"

And I did. And so did they. I thought the house had never looked so nice as we walked to the pizzeria. And then Carrina revealed her true genius.

When we arrived at the pizzeria, Carrina said in a devilish voice, "I think your sisters are big enough to sit at a table by themselves, don't you, Antonio?" She batted her eyelashes at me.

My sisters giggled.

"They want to be alone," Luisa whispered.

So alone we were. Or as alone as we could be with my sisters sitting at the next table, leaning over, trying to hear what we were saying. I took Carrina's hand. My sisters snickered. Self-conscious, I released her hand and smiled. "I can't believe they do anything you want," I announced.

"I have a younger sister," Carrina whispered. "I

learned long ago how to make her do what I wanted while making her think she was doing what she wanted."

"How much younger is she?" I bit into a slice of pizza.

"A year younger and a holy terror. She's always getting into my things. She's a real pain sometimes. I can't believe how much I miss her," she said.

"Miss her?" I asked. I wondered if her sister had died—like my papa.

Carrina choked on her peach tea. I was about to worry that she wasn't okay when she slapped herself on the chest and took a deep breath. "Sorry, I think the tea went down the wrong way. I meant that I miss my sister this minute. She's a sweetie." She looked toward the marble slab where the workers flattened the dough. "I love the aroma of fresh dough," she murmured.

"Tourists like to watch them work," I mused.

"I'll bet."

Using a long-handled peel, the cooks whipped the pizza in and out of the wood-burning oven. The pizzas came out thin and crunchy with an assortment of ingredients to tempt any customer.

"My papa used to manage a pizzeria," I said quietly.

She jerked her gaze around to me. "He did?"

I nodded. "Sometimes I'd help him, but not often. He wanted me to study, to do well in school. To go to the university. He was killed in a car accident. A couple of years ago now."

She placed her small hand over my larger one. "I'm so sorry."

I turned my hand over and intertwined our fingers. I heard my sisters giggle again, but I was determined to ignore them. I decided I needed to be honest with Carrina. "I don't have a lot of time. I don't have a lot of money. If I did, I would want to date you."

She touched my cheek, and I felt the warmth shoot through me.

"What are you doing now?" she asked.

"This isn't a date," I assured her. "You're buying. My sisters are here."

"But we're together. I like it," she said softly.

"Do you?" I asked, needing the reassurance. I had so little to offer.

She smiled warmly. "Yeah, I do." She leaned toward me. "I have an idea. Let's play tourist this afternoon. All of us, you, me, and your sisters. There's plenty to do that doesn't cost money."

"Tourists?" I echoed. "Why?"

"Most people never look at their hometowns. Today let's pretend that we've never seen Rome—and let's see it together," she suggested.

Her idea appealed to me. I couldn't remember the last time that I'd taken a moment to look at my city. Nor could I think of a single girl I'd ever known who would want to spend the day with four giggling kids just to be with me.

A tourist in my own city. Interesting. And I knew that with Carrina beside me, everything would look different anyway.

Eight

Carrie

I WAS LIVING on the edge, flirting with danger. I was also flirting with Antonio.

I knew that I was just putting off the inevitable, but I wanted to have some warm memories of time spent with him before he hated me.

And hate me he would once he learned of my deception.

Why couldn't he have been the obnoxious jerk that I first thought he was? Why did he have to be sweet and lonely?

Why did he have to make my heart flutter like the wings of a captured butterfly every time he looked at me? Perhaps because he was capturing my heart.

Crazy, I know. I barely knew the guy, but I knew him well enough to know that my plan to teach him a lesson had turned on me. I was the one being taught something.

That intolerance worked both ways—and before I judged, I should probably walk in the other guy's shoes.

Piazza di Spagna—Spanish Square—was crowded when we arrived. Not surprising since it was one of the most famous squares in Rome. Within the center of the square was the true lure of the area: the Spanish Steps.

"Antonio, can we go to the top of the steps?" Gabriella asked.

"Yes, but hold hands," he ordered. "And wait at the top for us."

I watched his sisters run up the steps. I was glad he'd let them go. I wanted a little time alone with Antonio here.

The square reminded me of a crooked bow tie. Beige-, cream-, and russet-colored houses lined the square, some with their shutters closed, others with the shutters open.

"Let's go look at the fountain," I suggested.

Antonio gave me a smile. "Okay."

He took my hand. His hand was larger than mine and so warm.

"Is there a reason you waited until your sisters were out of sight?" I asked, holding up our joined hands.

"My sisters would tease you," he explained, his face turning red.

I tightened my fingers on his. "Antonio, with five brothers my life has been one long series of jokes, teasing, and general aggravation."

His smile deepened. "I'll remember that." He glanced away briefly before meeting my eyes. "Actually, Carrina, since my papa died, I haven't had much time for girls. I'm not always certain what's appropriate."

"Just do what feels right. If I don't like it, believe me, I'll let you know," I assured him.

He laughed warmly. "You aren't shy."

"Nope. I believe you have to grab every moment of life and ride it for all it's worth." I tugged on his hand. "The fountain."

The fountain at the base of the Spanish steps—the Fontana della Barcaccia—was far from spectacular. So many people sat on its rim that it was almost hidden. The pressure from the aqueduct that fed the fountain was extremely low, so it had no grand spurts of water or spectacular cascades. Still, the shallow pool was worth viewing.

Especially with Antonio by my side.

"If I remember my history, Spain's ambassador had his headquarters on this square in the seventeenth century," Antonio muttered.

"That's what the guidebook said," I concurred.

"The guidebook?" he asked.

I refrained from rolling my eyes. I was going to give myself away if I wasn't careful. I'd almost blown it earlier when I'd confessed missing my sister.

"Yes, guidebook. Like I mentioned earlier, people don't pay a lot of attention to the sites of interest in their hometowns, so . . . I bought a guidebook, and my hobby this year is to see all the spots mentioned in the book," I explained—without actually lying. The one thing that I did not want was for Antonio to think I'd lied to him. Deceived him, yes—by omission. But I didn't think I'd ever actually lied. Well, except about my name.

"I think it would take more than a year to see everything in Rome," Antonio stated.

"I'll just see what I can," I said.

"And see the rest next year," he told me.

"No," I said quietly. "I just want to see as much as I can in a year. . . . That's my goal. If I don't see it then, I don't know if I ever will."

He paled and pulled me away from the fountain. "Are you dying?" he asked in all seriousness.

I saw the fear in his eyes, the worry, and the concern. He knew only too well that a life could be short. I rubbed his arm, trying to reassure him. "Oh no. No, nothing like that."

"Then why do you only have a year to see Rome?" he asked.

I began to weave an elaborate story through my mind—then ordered myself to stop. I couldn't lie. He was going to despise me as it was. I didn't need to add more fuel to the fire. "Next year I'll be going to school in America."

His brow furrowed. "You've been accepted into the Year Abroad program?"

I didn't say anything, didn't nod, didn't shake

my head, didn't say, *Well, yes, and I'm in it now.* But my silence and sudden need to tie my sneaker left the false impression that I was going to be a Year Abroad student next year. Perhaps he thought I didn't answer because I was sad to be thinking of leaving Rome for a year just when I'd met him. Or maybe I was getting too ahead of myself—or even flattering myself that he'd care. Still, I comforted myself that my answers couldn't be construed as lies—even though they were misleading. I had to guide us away from a potentially dangerous topic.

"Yes, I'm in the program, but let's not talk about that. I won't be leaving for a whole year."

That was the truth.

We started walking up the Spanish Steps. "Why would you want to leave Italy?" he asked. "Especially Rome. It's so amazing. The city, the sights, the food, the people."

I couldn't deny that I loved the fast-paced life of Rome. People here never seemed to slow down.

"It's not that I *want* to leave," I tried to explain. Then I decided to give up. I sighed. "Oh, Antonio, my leaving is a whole year away. Let's just enjoy now."

He gave me a hesitant smile as he quickened his pace so we could catch up to his sisters. "Maybe I will give you a reason not to go."

And I realized I was afraid that might happen. Knowing Antonio better would give me a reason to want to stay in Rome—but once he learned the truth, he would definitely want me to leave. He'd

85

probably buy the airline ticket himself—with what little money he had.

The exuberance and vitality of Rome shone in the outdoor markets. We had left the Spanish Steps and soon found ourselves immersed in a bustling area where vendors displayed the most unassuming vegetable as though it were a work of art. Stallholders called out their wares, luring Italians and tourists alike. Everything was brightly colorful and incredibly exciting. I loved listening to the hum of conversation and watching people haggle with the vendors over a price.

"I don't know how people do that," I said to Antonio as we walked along, watching a vendor gesturing frantically with his hands while a potential customer did the same.

"It's an art," he admitted. "I usually just pay whatever they ask."

"Looking at all these ripe fruits and vegetables is making me hungry," I announced.

He laughed. "I'll have to keep you away from the celery so we don't have a sword fight in the middle of the square."

I blushed, remembering our little joust in the kitchen. I don't know what had possessed me to tease him with a stalk of celery—I just knew I wanted to see him smile. "Why stop at celery?" I inquired. "I can turn any stalk into a handy weapon."

"Antonio, I'm hungry," Gabriella muttered.

Antonio rolled his eyes. "We just ate a little while ago."

"I'm thirsty," Luisa stated.

"Me too," the other sisters chimed in.

I could tell that Antonio was about to protest. I wanted to keep his sisters happy so he could enjoy the day. "I saw someone walking by with some gelato," I told them. "Why don't we see if we can find the shop?"

His sisters brightened up and started searching for the shop. Gelato—Italian ice cream—was a little different from American ice cream. I was becoming a bit addicted to it.

"The gelato will be my treat," Antonio said quietly beside me.

"Okay." I squeezed his hand.

"There's a shop!" Gabriella shouted, pointing toward a *gelateria*.

The inside of the ice cream shop looked pretty much like the ones at home. Inside a huge glass bowl various types of cones were stacked one inside another. A cylinder held spoons for those who wanted their gelato in a cup. The guy behind the counter wore a paper hat.

Antonio's sisters danced up and down in front of the glass display that revealed all the flavors of gelato.

"I don't know what kind I want," Gabriella stated.

"Me either," Luisa chimed in.

"We'll be here forever," Antonio muttered.

I decided it was time to take over. "First things

first. Everyone tell me what kind of cone you want." Once cones were selected, I quickly moved them on to the gelato. We had two chocolates, two vanillas. Antonio ordered coffee flavor, and I ordered rum and raisin. Sounded weird, but I'd become hooked on it. We walked out of the shop with everyone smiling brightly, licking their double scoops of gelato.

"Have you ever tried this flavor?" I asked Antonio.

He grimaced. "Frozen raisins? No."

I shoved my cone toward him. "Try it."

He shook his head.

"Come on, chicken," I taunted. "Cluck, cluck, cluck."

He narrowed his eyes. "I don't want it."

"Just one little taste—be adventurous," I insisted.

"One taste," he agreed.

I watched as his mouth neared my cone. He had a really great looking mouth. His lips appeared soft. I watched his tongue dart out to touch the gelato before his mouth closed around the pointed tip I'd created with my constant licking.

A warm sensation shimmied through me as I wondered what it would feel like to have those lips touch mine.

Dangerous thought, Giovani, I warned myself. *Those lips will never kiss you. All they'll do is tell you to get the heck out of Rome.*

Antonio straightened, and I watched as his face showed mild surprise. Then he licked his lips. "Very good."

"Want some more?" I asked. My voice sounded like I'd just lined my throat with sandpaper. What was wrong with me?

I watched him take another bite—and then I put my mouth right where his had been. Probably the closest thing to a kiss I'd ever experience with him. And it was cold.

But I was certain it wasn't as cold as his kiss would be once he learned the truth.

Nine

Antonio

I COULDN'T REMEMBER when I'd enjoyed an afternoon so much.

Carrina was incredible. So full of life. She had so much energy. And she knew how to handle my sisters.

When they started to whine, she made them laugh. When they grew tired of walking, she created games that made them forget they were walking. How far can you travel without stepping on a crack? Not far on the cobblestones, but still, the game distracted my sisters.

Distracted my sisters but kept my attention focused on Carrina. She'd pulled her dark hair back in a ponytail, and it bounced against her back as she walked. She did everything quickly as though she was afraid she would run out of time—and still have so much left to do.

She intrigued me as no one else ever had.

Through her eyes, I was seeing Rome as though for the first time.

We arrived at the Trevi Fountain, the largest and most famous fountain in Rome. I couldn't remember when I'd last been here. Waterfalls cascaded over huge stones. The main statue was Neptune, flanked on each side by a Triton with a sea horse. I had forgotten how magnificent the sculptures were at the Trevi Fountain.

My sisters squealed with delight and ran to the rim of the fountain.

"Look, Antonio," Gabriella yelled. "There's money in here!"

Holding Carrina's hand, I walked to the edge of the fountain. Coins littered the bottom.

"Legend says if a visitor tosses in a coin, he will one day return to Rome," I explained.

Carrina dug her hand into her pocket, turned her back on the fountain, and tossed a coin over her shoulder.

"Why did you do that?" I asked. "You're not a visitor."

She blushed and shrugged. "I was making a wish. You don't have to be a visitor to do that."

"What did you wish?" Mara asked.

Carrina touched the tip of Mara's nose. "I can't tell you, or it won't come true." She handed each of my sisters a coin. "Make a wish."

My sisters' coins plopped into the water and

91

floated to the bottom of the blue fountain.

Carrina held my gaze and pressed a coin into my palm. "Make a wish, Antonio."

"I haven't wished in a long time," I said quietly.

She smiled warmly. "Then you're long overdue, and it's bound to come true."

I grinned at her. Whenever she looked at me like she was daring me to step out of my shell—I wanted to do whatever she wanted. I sighed deeply. "One wish. I could wish for money. I could wish for power. Or I could wish for—"

"Don't say it, Antonio!" my sisters shrieked.

I turned and tossed the coin over my shoulder.

"What did you wish for?" Carrina asked.

I laughed and took her hand. "I thought it was supposed to be a secret."

"You can tell me," she whispered.

"I don't think so." How could I tell her my wish when it revolved around her?

"People at school have been talking about the American Year Abroad student," I told Carrina as we neared my house. I felt her hand tense inside mine.

"Oh, really," she mused. "I suppose she's still using the boys' bathroom."

I chuckled. "No. I think you were right that she was just nervous. No one mentions that mistake anymore. Those who have met her really seem to like her."

"Is that so?" she inquired.

"I'm thinking that maybe I judged her too harshly," I admitted. "Like you told me."

"Sometimes it's just hard when we don't know people. I don't know why, but we tend to think the worst of them," she explained.

"You're right. That's why I've decided that I want to meet her," I stated.

Carrina came to an abrupt halt. Her dark eyes were wide, her brow furrowed. "You want to meet her?"

I nodded. "I only catch a glimpse of Americans when I serve them at the trattoria. I think it would help me understand Americans if I met the student at my school."

Carrina shook her head. "I doubt that. I hear that she's very quiet and that she keeps to herself at school and barely lifts her head when she walks down the halls."

"Maybe she's just shy," I pointed out. Weird. Now I was defending the American? "Anyway, people at school seem fascinated by her."

Carrina smiled. "That's very nice. I won't worry about her so much anymore."

I smiled back, and we started walking again. My sisters rushed ahead and got to the house first. I wished that I didn't have to go to work that evening. I wanted to spend more time with Carrina.

As we reached my house, I remembered that she'd originally come over to talk. There hadn't been a spare moment of awkward silence all day between Carrina and me. I wasn't surprised that I hadn't remembered until now. "You said you came over to talk to me about something."

"We talked plenty today," she said with a laugh. "I'll see you, Antonio."

I wanted to ask her when and where and how and what. But I figured I'd see her soon at La Sera, or perhaps she would surprise me with another visit at the house. I had a feeling I shouldn't crowd her.

"Is Carrina your girlfriend now?" asked Gabriella, hands on her little hips.

"It's looking good," I told her with a smile.

Happy shrieks and giggles emanated all over the house.

Private Internet Chat Room

Carrie: I spent the afternoon with Antonio. We toured parts of Rome. This city is so beautiful and old and amazing. I hope you guys can come over during the year.

Dana: Hey, so he took the news okay that you're the American?

Carrie: I didn't tell him.

Robin: Oops! Carrie, you have to tell him.

Carrie: I know. I was going to tell him today, but I just couldn't.

Dana: You really like him, huh?

Carrie: Yeah. I like him a lot. Maybe even more than a lot. He hasn't spent a lot of time around girls because he works so much and has to take care of his sisters. When he learns the truth about me, it's going to be a double whammy. Not only did an American betray him—but the first girl he ever trusted deceived him as well.

Dana: That's a little melodramatic, Carrie—even for you!

Carrie: I don't know about that. I really think he's going to hate me.

Robin: Maybe he'll surprise you and be completely understanding.

Carrie: Yeah, in my dreams.

Robin: So what are you going to do?

Carrie: Haven't a clue. I don't have a script. How I wish I did.

Dana: Tell him the truth, Car. It's the best way and the only way. The longer you put it off, the worse it'll be.

Carrie: Don't I know it.

Ten

Carrie

I STRETCHED OUT on my bed and opened the book on Michelangelo. Perhaps I should have told Antonio that I was the Year Abroad student when he'd mentioned he wanted to meet her.

But as my brothers would say—I'd choked. Bonked. Blew it.

All I'd had to say was, *You're holding her hand and looking at her like you really like her.*

Yeah, that would have gone over well. He would have stared at me in shock and horror and told me I'd played him for a fool. And how could I have done that in front of his sisters?

Excuses, excuses.

Watching Antonio with his sisters had warmed my heart, reminded me of my brothers, my family. Reminded me of what was real, what really mattered, what was important. My own stupid ego, my own stupid lie was pathetic in the face of everything Antonio had heaped on his young shoulders.

I closed the book. So much for working on my research paper. I'd rather work at La Sera. I could help out, spend a little extra time with my aunt and uncle and Roberto, and see Antonio.

I arrived at my uncle's restaurant two hours later. Aunt Bianca was happy to have me for the day. I talked to my aunt and uncle in the back room for a little while, mostly about school and about the e-mails I'd gotten from my parents, and then I put on an apron and headed into the dining room. Antonio was serving a table for two. A guy and a girl. I wondered if he was thinking that he wished he could be that guy, taking his girl out on a real date to a trattoria. The thought made my heart squeeze for him.

Every time Antonio and I passed each other, he'd smile warmly at me—and my heart would do this crazy kind of flutter.

Not good, Giovani, I thought. *Not good at all.*

I was incredibly torn. I needed to tell him the truth. I wanted to keep my secret.

I thought of the gladiators who had fought in the Colosseum in Rome. I'd seen pictures that showed a gladiator with one arm tied to one horse, another arm tied to another horse. He was supposed to be strong enough to keep them from tearing him apart.

I figured terror had gripped him at that moment as he hoped he was strong enough. . . . I always imagined that he had been. I was a sucker for courage.

And sadly lacking it.

Antonio, I'm American. Three little words. How hard could they be to repeat, to acknowledge? Pretty dadgum hard when saying them meant that Antonio would never again smile at me.

Antonio had offered to walk me home. I was waiting for him out front. I had a plan. A stupid plan, but a plan all the same.

I was going to let him take me home. All the way home. To Elena's. Then he'd realize who I was. I wouldn't have to speak the words. He would just . . . know.

I'd pulled Elena's scooter out from beside the building. She was a great host sister, letting me borrow it all the time.

The front door opened, and the moment I had been dreading had finally arrived. I turned and faced Antonio.

He walked down the steps, his brow furrowed. "You have a scooter?"

I nodded jerkily. "It's a friend's. I just borrowed it. I thought you could ride in front and I could ride behind."

He smiled. "Okay. But you have to wear the helmet."

I worked it onto my head. He started to turn the

scooter around. I put my hand on his arm. "Actually, I live in that direction."

He stared at me as though I'd lost my mind. "But the other night we went in that direction." He pointed behind me.

"I know. I got confused." I released a stupid, silly girl laugh. "I didn't realize it until I came back for my ring."

Don't question me here, I pleaded silently.

He nodded and swung his leg over the scooter. I got on behind him and put my arms around him.

"Where do you live?" he asked.

I gave him Elena's address.

"Do you mind if we take a detour?" he inquired.

I welcomed the reprieve—a few more minutes before he hated me. "No, I don't mind," I assured him.

He turned on the scooter. It made its little buzzing sound. I tightened my hold on him. Then we were churning along the street, heading into the night.

"My papa used to bring me here," Antonio said quietly as we stood by one of the huge columns on the steps of the Pantheon.

Visiting hours were over, and we couldn't go inside. But the building didn't lose its majesty with the coming of night. Its huge, domed roof simply reflected the moonlight and the lights of Rome.

"I had forgotten," Antonio added. "Until today, when we pretended that we were tourists."

He took my hand and intertwined our fingers.

"Always be proud of your heritage, Antonio." He sighed. "That is what he always told me . . . and what I forgot."

Even in the darkness of the night I could see his sad smile. I didn't think he really wanted me to comment. I thought he probably just wanted someone to listen.

"Inside the Pantheon, the only light comes from a hole in the center of the dome," he explained. "My papa would show me everything. Explain everything. He didn't need a guidebook."

His fingers tightened on my hand. "I miss him, Carrina. I had forgotten how much. Today you helped me remember."

"Oh, Antonio." I touched his cheek and felt the dampness where a tear had fallen.

He turned away his face, and I could see him wiping his face in the shadows. Why did guys have to think that tears were a weakness? My mom cried, and she was the strongest person I knew.

"My papa loves his heritage too," I said softly.

Antonio smiled. "I would like to meet your papa."

My heart rammed against my chest. Impossible. But I did wish that Antonio could meet my dad. He'd like my father. I knew it. Family was incredibly important to my dad, and he always made time for us—no matter how busy he was, he was never too busy for us. Just like Antonio seemed to be with his sisters and mother. I smiled at Antonio. "Maybe someday you will meet him," I said.

Antonio squeezed my hand, then sighed heavily. "I don't know why I came here."

"To feel close to your father," I explained. "We all have a special place for remembering those we love."

"I didn't want to come alone," he confessed. "I hope you don't mind that I brought you."

"No. It means a lot to me that you wanted to share this place with me," I told him.

"You mean a lot to me, Carrina." He tugged on my hand.

I stepped closer. Antonio drew me against him, lowered his head, and kissed me.

I melted, from the top of my head to the tips of my toes.

And Antonio tasted wonderful. He felt wonderful . . . and I knew how Pinocchio had felt when the fairy had touched her wand to his head and turned him into a real boy—that nothing would ever be as wondrous as this moment.

Eleven

Carrie

ANTONIO APPARENTLY HAD no idea that Elena lived in the house that he'd dropped me off in front of last night. I was as relieved as I was tormented. And left with the searing memory of his kiss. He'd kissed me again before he left to walk the half mile to his own house. I watched him until he disappeared into the night, my fingers caressing my lips in awe and wonder.

Now, Sunday afternoon, I stretched out on my bed with Elena beside me. She'd brought in a stack of pop magazines, including *Uno* and *Tutto*. They were pretty much like the magazines I read at home. Music, movies, and rock stars.

"Isn't he a heartbreaker?" Elena crooned in English.

Heartbreaker? That sounded like something my mom might say—twenty years ago. Elena was taking

English in school. In Italy it was considered a foreign language, of course, but it still seemed so odd to me. I mean, I found it strange that anyone would think of English as a foreign language. It just seemed like it should be at least everyone's second language if not their first. I heard a little voice inside my head, chastising me for escalating the significance of English. The little voice sounded a lot like Antonio's.

But that aside, Elena wanted to practice her English—slang and sayings. She was already far advanced in grammar and proper usage.

I glanced at the glossy photo of the dark-haired guy. "We'd say *hot* instead of *heartbreaker*," I told her.

"*Hot?* Hot. Isn't he a hot?" She smiled at me. "Like that?"

I grinned at her. "Without the *a*. Just *hot*. Totally hot."

"Isn't he totally hot?" she repeated. *"Grazie."*

"Thank you," I corrected.

She laughed. "I forget to always speak English when we get going in conversation."

She turned the page, and I went back to reading an article on Madonna, of all people. There were more Americans in this Italian magazine than Italians.

I gave up on the article. I couldn't keep my mind on it. I just kept thinking about Antonio. Last night when he'd brought me to Elena's house, I had expected him to confront me—to know I was the Year Abroad student. My heart had been pounding so hard, I was afraid he could hear it. With Antonio's schedule, it made sense that he wouldn't be up on where everyone in his school lived or who was hosting the American. He clearly didn't pay much attention to who was who or who was doing what with whom.

Last night at the Pantheon had been incredible. Not just the kiss, but the whole moment of closeness. Antonio had revealed some pretty heavy stuff about his feelings. I was willing to bet that he'd never opened up to anyone like that before. A wounded soul reaching out. A kindred spirit seeking shelter. He'd confided in me, turned to me for comfort. Me, the one person who had betrayed him—he just didn't know it yet.

"Carrie, what's wrong?" Elena asked.

I snapped to the present and looked at her. "What?"

She furrowed her brow. "You looked sad totally."

"Totally sad," I said, gently correcting her. Then I shook my head. "Only I'm not sad." *Devastated* was a better word, but I couldn't admit that without explaining what I'd done. How quickly my plot for revenge had turned on me. "Italy has been an adjustment I wasn't expecting."

"In what ways?" she asked.

"I just thought I knew everything about Italy and Italians . . . and I'm learning that there's a lot that I didn't know." The explanation sounded stupid. I wasn't learning so much about Italians as I was learning too much about me.

*　　*　　*

Being a Year Abroad student didn't mean that you were the host family's guest. Rather, it meant you became part of their family—which meant, unfortunately, chores. Groan.

Keeping my room clean, doing my laundry, helping with meals, cleaning up after meals—pretty much life as it was lived back home. Of course, there was a lot less to clean up after a meal at the Pietra table because they didn't have my five brothers eating like pigs at a slop trough.

There was also a lot less food served. And shopping for it was kinda fun because I didn't go to a grocery store. I simply went to the market. It was like walking through a never ending produce section of the grocery store back home—except I was outside. Huge open tents marked off the vendors' areas and provided some shade. Of course, for a girl accustomed to one-hundred-degree days, I wouldn't have minded the sun.

But I loved the atmosphere. Local produce like grapefruit was packed into carts. And imported fruits like pineapple were also available.

Signora Pietra had given me a list of what she needed to prepare her meals for the next few days. She'd told me to pick up anything else that I thought I might like to try. I had several hours to myself before my host mother expected me back with the groceries. That meant I could explore to my heart's content all day.

I'd come alone. Elena's chore had been to head

to the meat market. We'd agreed to switch off next week. I wanted to experience every part of Rome that I could. No task was too menial, no chore—regardless of how much I complained—beneath me.

It was all part of this exciting adventure called being a Year Abroad student.

Uncharacteristically I walked slowly from stall to stall, examining the produce. The area was a pot-pourri of aromas. I picked up something that looked like a melon. I brought it to my nose, closed my eyes, and sniffed.

It smelled sweet and ripe. My mouth watered.

"Restocking your arsenal?" a deep voice asked.

My eyes flew open. I recognized that voice. My heart patted my ribs as I turned and faced Antonio. He looked incredible. He was wearing a black T-shirt and jeans.

I moved my hand up and down as though gauging the weight of the melon. "I recently acquired a cannon. Now I need some ammunition."

He laughed, deeply and richly. It was a really nice laugh. My gaze dropped to his lips, and I remembered the kiss he'd bestowed upon me. My body grew warm. Maybe it was one hundred and five degrees in the shade after all.

I had to get my mind off that kiss, off that night of intimacy when he'd shared so much of himself with me. "What are you doing here?"

He grinned. "I need some onions, peppers." His smile grew. "Celery with stronger stalks."

Now it was my turn to laugh. "I guess you've figured out that I have a flair for the dramatic."

"You do have a way about you, Carrina Gio," he admitted.

My stomach lurched at the butchering of my name, a name I'd given him. A reminder of the lie that created a chasm between us. A chasm only I was aware of. I could tell him the truth now—even though the arsenal was at his disposal. I could imagine him searching for, finding, and throwing rotten tomatoes at me.

He took my hand, and I shoved all thoughts of revealing the truth to the back of my mind. The middle of a produce market was not the place.

"What are you shopping for?" he asked.

I put the melon back, reached into my pocket, removed the list, and flicked it open. "Boring stuff. Small knives." I winked at him. "Carrots. Bullets." I gave him a pointed look. He was grinning. "Grapes." I shrugged. "Just a few things."

Suddenly shopping for produce really did seem incredibly boring. I laced our fingers together. "I have a crazy idea."

He shook his head as though reading my mind. "I have to leave for work in a few hours. I don't have time to play tourist."

"How about lazy bum?" I prodded.

His eyes widened. "What?"

Excitement was thrumming through me. I knew it was dangerous to spend more time with

Antonio. The more comfortable I became around him, the less I kept my guard up. The easier I let little slips of the tongue reveal what I needed to tell him up front. But he was here, unexpectedly, and so was I.

And what could a couple more hours together hurt?

"I saw a park on my way over here. Some kids were playing soccer. I was thinking of going over there and watching."

"Every Sunday there are professional soccer games—"

"No," I interrupted. "I like to watch people play for the love of the game, not money. They still have the dream of being something. Too many professionals just dream about how much money goes into their bank accounts."

"What about your shopping?" he asked.

"I can do it later." I tugged on his hand. "Let's be wild and crazy."

Wild and crazy was a relative experience. Holding hands, we walked toward the park I'd seen. We passed one of Rome's many drinking fountains.

"Thirsty?" Antonio asked me.

"A little."

We backtracked and stopped at the elaborate fountain, where the water poured out of the mouth of a stone image—some mythical god, I assumed; Juno, maybe. I sipped the water. It was naturally sweet and really good.

"Every time I drink this water, I'm amazed at how good it tastes," I remarked.

"Another gift from the ancient Romans," Antonio responded. "Don't you know that the water is piped down from the hills through a series of pipes and aqueducts that have changed little over the centuries?"

I'd somehow overlooked that little fact in my guidebook, but a true Italian would know. "Of course I know, and knowing just makes me appreciate the water all the more."

But more than the water, I loved the fountains. Etched in stone. So much more interesting than the electric water fountains we had in Mustang—where the water always tasted like rust.

Antonio carried a bag of oranges that I'd picked up at one of the stands before we'd begun our trek to the park. I had decided that a makeshift picnic was in order.

We reached the park and sat at the top of a knoll where we had a clear view of the playing field. Antonio sat on the ground with his back against a tree. I sat in front of him, my back to his chest, his arms around me.

Content. Incredibly content.

The kids playing soccer were probably around twelve. They wore uniforms, so I figured they were part of some organized league. Soccer was extremely popular in Italy.

My brothers and I played constantly. I was tempted

to go down to the field and help out, but I was too happy where I was. In the circle of Antonio's arms.

I heard his stomach growl. I laughed. "I know that sound."

I reached for the bag beside us, pulled out an orange, and began peeling off the rind.

"You always add special touches to our excursions," he murmured.

"I believe in living life to the fullest," I commented as I tore off a section of the orange. I twisted around slightly. "Open your mouth."

He did, and I slid the orange into his mouth. I watched as his tongue licked the outer edges of his lips. So much for trying not to think about the kiss. I slipped an orange section into my mouth. I needed to keep my mouth busy—otherwise it was going to lean forward and kiss Antonio.

Would that be so bad? a tiny voice inside my head asked.

No, it would be wonderful, but until I knew if his feelings for me could withstand the truth, I thought it was best if I didn't make any advances. Oh, what a tangled web I'd woven, so tangled that I was now caught in it.

I wanted Antonio to be my boyfriend. In a way, I felt like he was. I wasn't seeing any other guys in Rome. I wasn't even flirting with any guys at school. As far as I was concerned, there was only one Italian for me—and I was with him right now.

What would it hurt if I never told him the

truth? Plenty. It would hurt plenty—him and me. Him because our relationship would be a lie. And me because I would be hiding my heritage—a heritage I was very proud of. And with every day that passed, I knew that I increased the risk of him finding out about me from someone else. I had to be the one to tell him.

But the perfect moment just never seemed to be here. I fed him another section of orange. It was such an intimate thing to do—almost as intimate as kissing. But it didn't send warm shock waves through my system the way his kiss had last night.

When we were finished with the orange, I snuggled back against him and tried to watch the soccer game, but all I could think about was how wonderful it was to be here with Antonio. I wanted to share every moment of this year with him.

"Where do you go to school, Carrina?" he asked abruptly. "It's so crazy that I just realized I don't know."

My heart bounced against my ribs. Oh gosh, there was no way that I couldn't *not* lie.

"I mean," he continued, "you don't live that far from me, we shop at the same market. . . . It just seems like we should be going to the same school."

I knew that in Italy, students had a choice between the *liceo*, a technical institute, or a teacher-training college. I cleared my throat. "My mom's a teacher. I thought I'd follow in her footsteps." That wasn't a lie. I was planning to major in drama and get a teaching certificate when I attended college

111

back in Texas. And my mom was an English teacher at Mustang High.

"So you're already working on your teacher training," he murmured.

I felt terrible. I hated lying. I hated it so much! How I wished I could turn back time to that first day when I'd heard him putting down Americans. How I wished I'd marched up to him and told him he was wrong, that I would prove to him how great Americans were.

I wondered what would have happened. Perhaps he wouldn't have given me the chance to prove anything. Perhaps he would have written me off as a rude, silly girl.

I sighed and nodded slightly in answer to his question as I snuggled closer against him. Let him take that nonanswer for a yes. If he thought that, he wouldn't expect to run into me at his school. But how—how, how, how—was I going to explain my lies when he learned the truth? One lie perhaps he could deal with. But all of these half-truths? All I was doing was digging myself in deeper.

But what else could I do? Telling him the truth meant losing him. And that I couldn't bear.

We sat in silence for several long moments. I enjoyed the peacefulness of it. I didn't know how much longer I'd have.

"My father and I used to play soccer," Antonio said quietly.

I burrowed my head against his shoulder. It

was another moment when I thought my silence was needed more than any trite words I could offer.

He brushed his cheek against mine. "Have you ever lost someone you loved?"

I shook my head. "I've been lucky."

"Carrina, turn around," he urged gently. "I have something for you."

A kiss. He was going to kiss me. I licked my lips. I tasted like orange. But then, so would he.

I turned around until I could face him. He reached behind his neck and lifted a chain over his head. On the end of it dangled a gold medallion. He slipped the necklace over my head. I cradled the medallion in the palm of my hand and studied the man who appeared to be hiking.

"It's Saint Christopher," Antonio said solemnly. "He is the patron saint of all travelers."

I lifted my gaze to his. "Antonio, I can't accept this."

He closed his hand around mine, pressing the medallion against my palm. "Please, Carrina. For when you travel to America."

I touched his cheek. Tears burned my eyes. "I'm not leaving for a whole year."

"Then let him protect you wherever you travel. Even in Rome it can be dangerous. I don't want you to get hurt."

I knew it was wrong to accept so precious a gift. But Antonio looked at me with such hope in his eyes that I absolutely couldn't say no.

Nor did I want to. The gift was precious to me. So, so precious.

Later that evening, in my room at my host family's house, I sat on my bed and leaned against the brass-railing headboard. I held the Saint Christopher medallion in my palm.

Was this how teens in Rome indicated that they were going steady?

Antonio and I hadn't even had what I'd consider a real date. But somehow that didn't matter. When I was with him, I was incredibly happy—except for that little voice at the back of my mind that kept nagging me. A little voice that kept reminding me that I wasn't the girl he thought I was.

Would he have given the medallion to an American girl? Probably not.

I knew that I had no business accepting his gift. But I'd been powerless to say no. I didn't want to hurt him, and I could tell that he would have felt rejected if I hadn't taken the medallion.

All that aside, I wanted it. I wanted something that had once belonged to Antonio.

I slipped the chain over my head and felt the medallion grow warm just below my throat. I pulled my small jewelry box closer. I needed to find something to give him.

I lifted the lid. A ballerina dressed in pink sprang upright and began to twirl as music tinkled into the room. Corny, I know, but I'd had the jewelry box since I was eight. When you were eight, twirling ballerinas were romantic. At sixteen they were a reminder of exactly how much you'd matured.

I'd brought only my favorite jewelry (not that I had so much in the first place). I picked up a charm bracelet. I couldn't quite envision Antonio wearing a charm bracelet, and the charms, which included the state of Texas, the Alamo, and a longhorn, revealed more about me than I wanted Antonio to know at this moment.

I set aside the bracelet and picked up a necklace. The silver chain was thick, but the heart-shaped locket that dangled from the chain—I really couldn't see that around Antonio's neck.

What was I thinking to even consider giving Antonio something in exchange for the Saint Christopher? I was going to have to give it back to him. When he learned the truth about me, he was going to demand that I give it back to him.

I would understand completely.

I stretched out on my bed and shoved my pillow beneath my head. I watched the ballerina twirl—and thoughts swirled through my head.

Tell Antonio the truth—and lose him.

Keep my secret—keep Antonio.

But did I truly have Antonio when he didn't know everything there was to know about me?

Twelve

Antonio

O N WEDNESDAY NIGHT Carrina and I sat at
the café near the trattoria. Our shift had
ended, and we'd come here to unwind. We had our
usual order. . . . Only this time we shared the
tiramisú, one of my favorite desserts.

I'd never shared anything with a girl until
Carrina had made me sample her rum-and-raisin
gelato. I liked how close it made me feel to her. I
thought I could tell Carrina anything, and she
would understand.

"I have decided that the Year Abroad student is
a myth," I announced. I sipped my espresso and
gazed at her over the rim of my cup.

She stilled, her piece of *tiramisú* halfway to her
mouth. "What?"

I set down my cup and leaned forward.

"People tell me about her, but I never see her—not in the hallways, not in any classes, not in the boys' bathroom."

A corner of her mouth tilted up. "I thought she'd stopped frequenting boys' bathrooms."

I shrugged. "That's what I heard. So where is she? You said two of your friends were in the Year Abroad program. Don't they have to go to class?"

"Of course they do," she admitted, but she seemed a little agitated.

I wondered if she missed her friends. To have two friends go away. "Do you miss them?" I asked.

"Who?"

"Your friends," I prodded.

She smiled softly. "Yeah, I do."

At that moment I realized that I knew so little about Carrina. I'd never met her family. Had never seen her with any friends. Was she as lonely as I was? "What are they like?"

"Well . . . Robin is the one in London. I call her dare-me-to-do-anything Robin. But she doesn't really like herself, and she wants to change while she's away," she explained.

"What does she want to change?" I inquired.

"The way she talks. She wants to be sophisticated." She shrugged. "But I like her the way she is."

"And your other friend?"

"Dana." Her smile grew. "She wants to fall in love while she's in Paris. She dated a totally unromantic guy for a while, and she's determined to have an all-out romance while she's in Paris. Unfortunately she keeps running into a guy from our school who's also in the program. He's driving her crazy."

"Why?" I asked. I wasn't sure it was a bad thing for a guy to drive a girl crazy. Didn't that mean she was always thinking of him?

"Because he's interfering with her plans to fall for a French guy," she stated.

"Only if she lets him," I pointed out.

She glanced around the restaurant as though she was looking for spies. Then she leaned forward, a conspiratorial glint in her eyes. "Truthfully, I think she likes him. And she doesn't want to. He's not French. He's Am . . . uh . . . a guy that we went to school with."

"You are very close to them," I murmured.

"Extremely." She leaned back. "I can tell them anything—the very worst thing about me—and they'd still be my friends."

"You're lucky. A lot of my friends didn't know what to say when my papa died. I still have a few friends, but it's hard to lose friends," I surmised.

"Well, I haven't lost Dana and Robin. They're just gone for a while. But in a year we'll be back together," she said.

"Until you leave for America," I reminded her.

She nodded. "Right."

I slapped my hand on the table. "I need to meet this American student at my school."

Carrina eyed me. "Why?"

"I want to know that they are nice in America. That they will treat you right while you are away," I told her. She would be so far from home, away from all that she knew. I could not imagine the courage that would take—to leave everything you knew and loved to experience another culture. That was part of the reason I'd given her my Saint Christopher medallion.

Carrina was looking at me with a strange expression, an expression that told me she thought what I'd just said was nice and sweet. "Americans are nice, Antonio. Maybe not all of them, but I've met some Italians who weren't nice," she told me.

"Like who?" I asked.

"Like the pedestrian who stepped onto the street in front of me this afternoon because she was too busy talking on her cell phone to pay attention to where she was going," she said. "I had to swerve to miss her and almost lost control of the scooter." She touched my medallion and smiled warmly. "Thank goodness I had this to protect me."

I was also glad that she had it. "Maybe it was the American," I suggested.

Carrina laughed, and I laughed too.

"I really want to meet this American," I told her. "How do I find her?"

"You'll find her eventually," she said.

"I hope so. I feel like I've been unfair to Americans, so I want to talk with one when I'm not serving her food," I explained.

She smiled. "You know, Antonio, if you're not careful, you might make me jealous."

I laughed. "If you are jealous, then you must like me."

She placed her hand over mine. "I do like you, Antonio. Very much."

She removed the puzzle ring from her third finger. Then she took my hand. I held my breath while she slid it onto my little finger.

She gave me a wry look. "It won't protect you from anything."

I lifted my hand and studied the ring. It wasn't delicate. It could actually be a guy's ring. It looked like several figure eights woven together. "I don't know what to say, Carrina. I thought this ring was important to you."

"You're more important," she assured me.

The next afternoon I sat on my bed at home, turning the ring on my finger over and over. Was Carrina my girlfriend now? I didn't know how to know if I had a girlfriend. Were we supposed to announce it—or did it just happen?

I wasn't sure, but I did know that I felt the need to celebrate. She didn't just like me. She liked me very much! And I was important to her.

Her acknowledgment called for a celebration of great magnitude. Fireworks. A national holiday. And if I couldn't get that—at least a night off from work. A night off with Carrina.

If she was willing. She'd given me her phone number. I stared at the phone. I'd never had a real date with a girl. Even though I was certain Carrina would say yes, I was still nervous.

Sweat beaded my brow. And my hand was actually shaking slightly as I picked up the phone and dialed her number.

When a girl answered, my mouth went dry. Why hadn't I thought to have a glass of water nearby?

"Uh . . . uh, is Carrina there?" I asked.

"Just a minute."

I heard the phone click as she set it down. That must have been her younger sister. Funny how she sounded older than I would have expected. I guessed that I was just so used to my younger sisters that I expected all girls who weren't my age to sound silly on the phone.

"Hello?"

My heart slammed against my ribs as I heard Carrina's voice.

"Carrina, it's Antonio."

"Antonio! How are you?"

"Well. I . . . uh . . . I was wondering if you'd like to go out on a date—a real date—Saturday night. We could both ask off from work," I suggested.

"A date?"

"I was thinking the opera. There is an open-air showing at some of the Roman ruins. I thought you could check it off your list of sites to see this year." I was rambling. I knew I was rambling. Why was I so nervous when I knew that she liked me? We'd exchanged tokens of affection—or were they just tokens of friendship?

"The opera," she said softly. "I'd like to see the opera."

"So you'll go with me?" I asked. I wanted to make sure she was saying yes to the date.

"Yes," she responded.

I closed my eyes tightly and pressed my fist against my chest. Yes! She'd said yes.

She agreed to call the Romano family and ask for Saturday night off. Since I was working later that evening, I decided to ask in person.

I arrived at the trattoria more than nervous. What if they said no?

Signore Romano was setting huge pots of water on the stove when I arrived. I figured we went through a ton of pasta every night.

I rubbed my damp palms on my trousers. "Signore Romano?"

He turned and raised a brow. "Antonio, you're early tonight."

"Yes, sir. I wanted to ask you if I could have Saturday night off," I told him. Then added, "This Saturday."

He slowly ran his gaze over me as though he wanted to get a measure of the kind of person I was. He nodded. "Yes, you can have Saturday night off." He quickly held up a finger. "But you take care with Carrina's heart."

I jerked my head back as though he'd slapped me. "You know that I'm taking Carrina out?"

He jabbed two of his fingers toward his eyes. "I have eyes! I see the way you look at her, the way she looks at you. Then she calls and tells me she is to go out with you. I don't want to see her get hurt."

"I would never hurt her," I announced adamantly. "I like her. A lot."

"Sometimes, Antonio, that is not enough," he said quietly.

Did he want me to love Carrina? I couldn't figure out why he cared. After all, she was just an employee here—like me. I didn't know what to say to him.

Signore Romano suddenly smiled brightly and slapped my shoulder. "Have a good time Saturday."

He turned back to his boiling water. Strange. He'd almost acted like I was taking out his daughter.

Private Internet Chat Room

Carrie: I don't know whether this goes under the heading of getting better or worse. But I have a date—a real date—with Antonio on Saturday night.

Dana: Cool!

Robin: Awesome!

Carrie: Here's what I'm thinking. We'll have this one night of perfection, and when it's over, I'll break the news to him that I'm American.

Dana: You'll ruin the evening.

Carrie: But if we have a good time, maybe he'll be more forgiving.

Robin: I think you're asking for trouble.

Carrie: I know. I probably should tell him before we go out. . . . But I want this night with him.

Dana: Maybe you'll never have to tell him. We're only going to be abroad for a year. Tell him before you go back home.

Carrie: Easier said than done. I'm playing dodge Antonio at school, and it's growing wearisome. Sooner or later he'll learn the truth, and I want him to hear it from me.

Robin: Then tell him the day after your date. After all, I was honest with Kit . . . and now he's my boyfriend.

Robin had told us a couple of days ago that Kit had broken up with his girlfriend and declared his serious like for Robin. I was totally happy for her. But her situation was way different from mine.

Carrie: But you didn't deceive Kit. You just hid your accent from him. Not your identity.

Thirteen

Carrie

A REAL DATE with Antonio required something special. Something definitely Italian.

With Elena in tow, I headed to the Mercato di Via Sannio. It was an open-air market where random stalls were set up to sell all sorts of wares inexpensively—including clothes and shoes. My budget was horrifyingly limited.

Department stores—*grandi magazzini*—were rare in Rome. The city had two shopping centers. As for malls—forget it. If they existed within the city limits, neither Elena nor I knew the whereabouts. And that was fine with me. I thrived on the open-air markets. The bustle, the bickering, the vendors trying to draw you closer so they could sell you something that you probably didn't really need or truly want.

Browsing was a totally cool experience. Even with all the noise and excitement in the air, I didn't feel the need to rush. I just wanted to find the perfect outfit to wear for Antonio.

"So who is this mystery guy?" Elena asked as she picked up a dress, then put it back on the stack resting on the table.

I hadn't told her that I'd been seeing Antonio. I was afraid she might say something to someone at school who might say something to someone else, and eventually Antonio would hear that he was dating the Year Abroad student. Wouldn't that just thrill him to death?

I picked up a colorful, flowing skirt and held it against my waist. The hem touched me at midcalf. Red and black designs swirled over the cloth. "I'm not ready to talk about him yet, Elena. I'm afraid to jinx it."

She smiled. "I know what you mean. Okay, you'll tell me when you're ready. You can tell me what he looks like, though, right? Is he totally hot?"

I laughed, clutching the skirt to my chest as I thought of Antonio. I knew I had a dreamy look on my face. I just couldn't help it. He did that to me. "Totally, totally hot. He's tall. Dirty blond hair, blue eyes. He's so cute. And so very nice."

She squealed. "I can't wait to meet him when he comes to get you tonight."

I'd been thinking about that problem, wondering how I was going to avoid her seeing Antonio.

Or worse, him seeing her. I'd considered walking to the end of the block and waiting for him there, but I was afraid I might miss him or he might not see me. There was no way around this. I was going to have to come clean.

I put the skirt aside. "Elena, I'm going out with Antonio."

Her eyes nearly popped out of her head. "Antonio Donatello?"

I nodded.

"That's wonderful. I remember that you asked me about him, but I didn't know you wanted to date him," she exclaimed.

"Elena . . ." I felt tears sting my eyes.

She took my hand. She looked worried. "What's wrong?"

"He doesn't know I'm American," I blurted out.

Her mouth dropped open. She snapped it shut. She waved a hand through the air. "How could he not know?"

"This skirt is your color!" a man's voice announced.

I jerked around. The heavyset vendor was clutching the skirt I'd been looking at. "You want?" he asked.

I shook my head. "I'm still thinking about it." Of all the places to explain my stupidity. I grabbed Elena's arm and led her away from the stalls. People brushed by us.

"It's been awful," I finally admitted. "I over-heard Antonio putting down American girls, so I decided to teach him a lesson. I was going to let him think I was Italian, flirt with him a little, get him to like me . . . then tell him I was an American. Only it backfired."

"Backfired?" she repeated.

"Turned on me," I tried to explain. Sometimes no language had the right words.

"Because you ended up really liking him," she stated with understanding.

I nodded. "A lot. And I know that it's going to hurt him when he learns the truth."

"He goes to our school," she pointed out.

"And that has been an absolute nightmare. I'm constantly peering around corners, ducking into classrooms where I don't belong. A couple of times he's come so close to seeing me. I'm just grateful we don't have any classes together," I admitted.

"Ah, so that's why you have the reputation for keeping to yourself! I can't believe you managed to avoid him."

"Neither can I." I wrapped my hand around her arm. "Elena, I didn't tell you about him because I was afraid you might accidentally mention what I'd done to someone—and he'd hear about it. I have to be the one to tell Antonio what an idiot I am."

She moved her fingers across her lips as if she were zipping up a dress. "My lips are sealed."

"Grazie," I said with meaning.

"When are you going to tell him?" she asked.

"I don't know. I've tried a couple of times, but I

just don't know how to say it," I confessed.

"You'd better be the one to open the door tonight. If he sees me or my parents—I don't know him well, but he knows who I am," she told me.

"He brought me home one night. I was afraid then that he'd figure it out," I told her.

She shook her head. "We have a class together, but I don't think he knows where I live."

I sighed deeply. "I know I have to tell him soon. The longer I put it off, the worse it's going to be."

As we walked back to the stalls, though, I was afraid I'd waited way too long already.

I was determined that tonight would be the night when I told Antonio the truth. I could see the moment so clearly in my mind.

We would be standing outside Elena's house. The aria from the opera still circling on the air around us.

Antonio, I would whisper softly. *This was the most incredible night of my life, and I want to give you something that you've wanted for a long time.*

He would lean closer and say, *You know what I want?*

Yes, I would admit. *You want to meet the American Year Abroad student.* I would throw out my arms. *Ta da! I'm her!*

At which point I somehow ended up with a pot of spaghetti sauce dumped over my head, and Antonio was nowhere to be seen.

I groaned as I stared at my reflection in the mirror. "It's not going to be pretty."

But, I thought with a little satisfaction, *I* looked pretty. Pretty good anyway. My trip to the market had paid off. I'd returned to that first stall and purchased the red-and-black skirt. Then I'd found a red top with spaghetti straps and sheer shirt to go with it. I'd discovered the most adorable belt made out of ancient-looking coins. They were linked together, and when I hooked the belt, a chain of coins dangled down my side.

I was wearing my hair loose, like a curtain flowing past my shoulders. On one side I'd clipped a barrette that had tiny red flowers. I thought it made me look . . . well, exotic. I'd used powder on my nose and a touch of shimmery pale eye shadow on my lids and a little mascara.

I wanted to give Antonio a night to remember. Because it might very well be our last.

Fourteen

Antonio

CARRINA LOOKED . . . incredible. I could hardly take my eyes off her as we sat among the Roman ruins. At the front was a stage, and behind it was what remained of columns. It created a magnificent backdrop to the opera.

Sitting in the audience, Carrina and I held hands. I'd been disappointed that I hadn't been able to meet any of her family. When I arrived to pick her up, she'd told me that they'd gone out for the evening. Carrina's life had so many pieces that I didn't know anything about. Her family, her friends, her school, her hobbies and interests. I did know she enjoyed opera. Her expression was one of . . . rapture.

She was totally absorbed in *Aida* as the hero sang of his love for an Ethiopian slave. And I was totally absorbed in Carrina. She was the main piece of the puzzle—and even without knowing everything about the other aspects of her life, I knew that I cared for her deeply.

I'd never felt this way about a girl. I wanted to see her every day. I loved talking with her. Her voice was music, her smiles were sunshine, and her laughter touched me as nothing else ever had.

Okay, heavy thoughts. I'll admit I was a little frightened that I was having them. I knew guys who let girls wrap them around their little finger. I'd never expected to be one of those guys.

But whatever Carrina wanted to do, I wanted to do. Be a tourist? I'd be a tourist. Understand Americans? I'd try.

I just might do anything for the girl.

My mama had refused to purchase a car after my papa was killed—not that we could really afford one. So my traveling was usually using the underground system—the Metropolitana—or the city buses. Tonight I wished that I did have a car.

Although Carrina didn't seem at all bothered by the fact that we had to use the Metropolitana, then a bus, and then our legs to get to her house. True, the bus had dropped us off only a block or so from where she lived, but I would have preferred being able to drive her to the front door.

Still, there was something romantic about the night. It was late, and the streetlights cast a hazy glow over everything. It seemed the most natural thing in the world to hold Carrina's hand—as I had for most of the evening. I loved the way her small hand fit inside mine. So trusting. It made me feel complete.

"You know, it's the funniest thing," I began.

She peered over at me. "What is? My hair? My outfit?"

I smiled. "No, your house. A girl from my school—Elena Pietra—used to live there. When I picked you up earlier, I realized that was why the house looked familiar to me from the outside. I'd passed it a few times, and the people I was with pointed out that was where Elena lived. I didn't know she'd moved. But then again, I know so little about my classmates."

"Were you and Elena friends?" she asked.

I shook my head. "No, we have a class together this year, but that's all."

Carrina squeezed my hand. "I really enjoyed the opera."

"Is that the reason I have a soggy handkerchief in my pocket?" She'd cried when the hero and heroine had died together. Although saying she cried was putting it mildly. More like sobbed her heart out.

Carrina sighed deeply, and I knew she was still thinking of that tragic ending. Strange how I understood that even though there were so many things that I didn't know about her.

"I'm still getting shivers running down my back," she said softly.

"The air is cool. Maybe you're just cold," I teased.

She glanced over at me and eyed me thoughtfully. "Oh, Antonio, it's the night, all right, but it has nothing to do with the temperature." She squeezed my hand. "Everything was just wonderful."

"I'm glad," I admitted. "I was so nervous about tonight."

She smiled warmly. "Why?"

I ran a hand through my hair. Dare I reveal the truth? I dared. "This was my first date." My first real date anyway. I didn't count walking girls home from school before my papa had died. Or sitting in the library with a girl with our noses in textbooks.

Her smile withered, and she stopped walking. A sadness touched her eyes. "Then that makes tonight extra special."

"You made it extra special, Carrina."

I hadn't planned to kiss her so soon. I'd planned to wait until we reached her house—but if being with Carrina had taught me one thing, it was to seize the moment.

I placed my hands on either side of her face. Her eyes were such a deep brown. I felt like I was swirling within the chocolate depths.

"I like you so much," I said hoarsely.

Then I pressed my lips to hers. She stepped closer to me and wound her arms around my neck. The kiss took on a life of its own.

All my senses burst into life as they never had before. I tasted the sweetness of Carrina's lips— more flavorful than the most expensive truffle. I inhaled her flowery sent. My fingers skimmed along her silky cheek. I heard her soft moan.

And even though my eyes were closed, I could see her so clearly—this girl who had touched my life and changed it in ways I'd never thought possible.

Fifteen

Carrie

I LAY ON my bed, curled on my side. Psychiatrists call it the fetal position. People go into it when they're afraid, they miss their mothers, or the pain is too great to bear.

I was experiencing all three, but most of all, I hurt.

Hot tears streamed along my cheeks. My chest ached as though someone had managed to put a tight rubber band around it. My head throbbed. And my heart . . . my heart felt like it was breaking.

Five of the most beautiful words in the world. *I like you so much.*

Only Antonio didn't know that he didn't mean them.

He couldn't possibly feel that way about me because he didn't know who I really was. He thought I was a quirky Italian girl who was obsessed with sightseeing. He thought my family lived in this house. He thought the Romano family was my employer.

He didn't know that the reason he'd never seen the Year Abroad student at his school was because she—or rather I—was wearing myself out trying to avoid him. In the last week I'd had too many close calls. Coming out of the girls' bathroom one second after Antonio walked by the door. Turning to find my nose almost touching his back.

It was getting harder and harder to hide from him at school because he was becoming more insistent on finding me. Why did he care so much about finding a girl that he'd admitted he thought was stupid? Curiosity?

I couldn't help but think I'd brought his obsession with the YA student on myself—blathering about how great Americans were and how important it was to walk in their shoes—well, right now the shoes were pinching my toes.

I squeezed my eyes shut. Tears leaked between my lids. Why hadn't I told him the truth about me sooner? I'd never been chicken. I'd never been afraid. I'd never been mean. Now I was all three.

After he'd declared his feelings, there was absolutely no way I could reveal the truth. And after that incredible kiss that had melted my bones, I wasn't certain that I could have spoken if I'd tried.

But it was more than that. I didn't want to see the soft look in his blue eyes turn hard.

When he spoke my name—Carrina—my name just rolled so provocatively off his tongue. It sent warm shivers along my spine.

What was I going to do?

I'd fallen for Antonio—and I knew if I told him the truth now, I'd lose him . . . forever.

On Monday morning I was called into the main office at school. The academic adviser wanted to see me. I couldn't figure out why. My grades were good. I was turning in all my assignments. I liked my classes. I wasn't having any problems with the teachers. All in all, her summons made no sense whatsoever. At least this was one thing American schools and Italian schools had in common. Kids got called to the office and didn't have a clue as to the reason.

The receptionist sat behind a huge counter, clicking away at her computer. I stared at plaques on the wall—totally uninterested in their significance. As I waited for Signorina DiMitri, the academic adviser, I reflected on the decision I'd made the night before.

Sunday I hadn't gone to work at La Sera. Neither had Antonio called me. That had bummed me out a little. After his declaration Saturday night, I figured he'd want some contact. I didn't want to sever all ties with him. I wanted to hear his voice. But I thought seeing him in person would be too incredibly hard.

I had spent Sunday doing a lot of soul searching. Not exactly what I'd planned when I decided I wanted to spend a year in Rome. By the time I crawled into bed, I'd gathered my courage.

Today after school I was going to tell him the truth about me. I was going to go to his house and confront my fears, face my misgivings, and deal with his anger.

Signorina DiMitri stepped out of her office and smiled broadly. "Thank you for coming, Carrie."

I held up the note she'd sent to my first-class teacher. "Back home when we get a note from the office, we don't have a choice."

She laughed. "It's the same here."

"So what did you need?" I asked.

"Well, I have a special favor to ask. As you know, English is a foreign language here. We teach formal English, but Signora Calendri wants to take advantage of your presence in our school. She was hoping you'd consent to teach her students some of the American phrases that you wouldn't find in a textbook."

A whole slew of phrases went through my mind. None of them would be in any textbook—American or Italian. I shrugged. "Sure."

"Wonderful!" She gazed past me, and I heard footsteps as someone else came into the office. "Here's your escort."

I turned, and my heart slammed against my ribs.

Antonio!

Joy lit his face momentarily. Then he furrowed his brow as though he suddenly realized that I shouldn't be here at his school.

"Antonio, have you met our Year Abroad student?" Signorina DiMitri asked.

His mouth dropped open, and he stared at me. The color drained from his face. "No," he replied hesitantly, his gaze never leaving my face. I knew all

140

the blood had drained from my face too. I probably looked like a ghost. "I have wanted to . . . but our paths have not crossed," he added stiffly.

"Well, then, let me introduce you. Antonio, this is Carrie Giovani, from Mustang, Texas. Carrie, Antonio Donatello is in Signora Calendri's English class during this hour. We thought it would be easier for you to find her class if someone walked you there."

I heard a phone ring in the distance.

"Excuse me," Signorina DiMitri said. "I have to get the phone, but you can go on to the class."

She walked back into her office, but neither Antonio nor I moved. He looked like he might be close to barfing.

"Carrie?" he rasped. I heard the disbelief in his voice.

My chest ached. My mouth was dry as I responded in English. "Carrie is short for Carrina."

"You're the Year Abroad student?" He looked like he was in pain. I wanted to put my arms around him and comfort him. "You're American?"

I nodded. My stomach roiled. "I can explain."

"You can explain?" he repeated. "You can explain? You can explain making a fool of me?"

"I didn't mean for it to be like that—," I began.

"I never want to see you again!" he shouted. "Ever!"

I watched him storm out. Then I heard the sound of my heart shattering, and I knew what it was to lose someone you loved.

Sixteen

Carrie

I PUTTERED ALONG the street on Elena's scooter. Destination: La Sera.

I had explained to Signorina DiMitri that I needed a couple of days to come up with some examples of American slang. She'd been thrilled with my enthusiasm for the project and had immediately gone to tell Signora Calendri of the change in plans.

I hadn't seen Antonio since he stalked out of the office. After school Elena had told me that Antonio had never returned to English class. I remembered that they had one class together. Why hadn't it occurred to me that it was English? Why hadn't I asked Antonio what classes he took? Why hadn't I asked Elena what class they shared?

Would that knowledge have made a difference? My head said no, but my heart was searching for ways I could have altered this morning. Oh, to have a time machine . . . to go back just twenty-four hours. If only I'd gone to his house yesterday. He'd probably never believe now that I had planned to tell him the truth.

I'd waited too long. Now I had so much more to explain. If only he'd hung around long enough to hear what I had to say.

I parked the scooter outside the restaurant. As I removed my helmet, I realized that my hands were trembling. I took a deep breath and marched up the steps as though I were going to an execution. No matter how many different ways I ran the story through my mind, I was the bad guy.

I, who usually played the heroine. Juliet. Maria in *The Sound of Music*. Eliza Doolittle in *My Fair Lady*.

Now I truly felt like the only villain I'd ever played: Cruella De Vil.

I opened the door and peered into the restaurant. Aunt Bianca was placing white starched tablecloths over the tables. She turned and smiled brightly. "Carrina!"

She held out her arms, and I went into her embrace. I needed to feel the love of family. I wrapped my arms around her and hugged her tightly.

"Ah, Carrina," she crooned. "I did not think you were going to work this week."

I leaned back and met her gaze. "I'm not. I just need to talk to Antonio."

She wrinkled her brow. "Antonio quit."

Shocked, I stepped back. "What?"

She moved her hand through the air as though she couldn't explain. "He just called your uncle Vito and said he would not work here anymore."

"Oh no!" My heart sank. I dropped into a nearby chair and buried my face in my hands. I knew Antonio couldn't afford not to work. How he must hate me to give up what he so desperately needed.

Aunt Bianca sat beside me and rubbed my back. "What is wrong, Carrina?"

I raised my gaze. "Oh, Aunt Bianca, my brilliant plan turned out to be not so brilliant. Antonio liked me. I liked him. But he thought I was Italian. And today at school he found out I'm American."

"Ah," she said on a soft sigh.

"He hates me," I blurted out. "I guess he quit because he doesn't want to see me anymore." I touched her arm. "You have to let him come back to work here."

"Not if he hurt you, Carrina," she stated adamantly.

"He didn't," I promised her. "I hurt him."

I remembered the first time I ever had a lead in a play. I was in the sixth grade, and I was Joan of Arc. I was totally nervous, shaking so badly that my armor—paper clips linked together to form my chain mail—rattled. I'd called myself the Maid of New Orleans instead of Orléans . . . I think because we'd gone to New Orleans for vacation that summer. Everyone had laughed. I'd been mortified.

I wanted to share these embarrassing moments with Antonio. Make him smile; more, make him laugh.

But I didn't think he'd give me a chance to share much before he went postal at my presence.

Taking a deep breath, I knocked on his door. I was hoping one of his sisters might answer it and I'd have a bit of a reprieve. Then I wished that he would open it so I could get the worst moment of my life over with.

Antonio answered the door. Well, one wish had come true.

My breath backed up in my lungs. I'd never seen so much hurt reflected in a pair of eyes before.

Anger flared in his eyes briefly, and he started to shut the door. I slammed my palm against it. "Antonio, I have to talk to you."

"Carrie, isn't it?" he asked, saying my name as though it were repugnant. "I don't think we have anything to talk about."

"You don't have to quit working at La Sera," I blurted out.

He narrowed his eyes. "Are you quitting?"

I swallowed. "I never really worked there. Signora Romano is my father's sister. I was just helping out that first night."

I saw the fury roll over his face. "They knew? They knew the trick you were playing?"

"No!" I responded quickly. "They told me to keep the fact that I'm American to myself because the tourists like the real thing to serve them. So I kept quiet."

"Why, Carrina?" he rasped. "Why did you deceive me?"

Tears stung my eyes. The moment of truth had come, and it sounded so . . . so lame. "I overheard you putting down American girls that first day we met. You said they were selfish and silly. I thought if you got to know me—thinking I was Italian—that when you discovered I was American, you'd realize that you were wrong about Americans."

"Instead I learned that I was absolutely right," he said harshly.

I nodded. "Yeah. You were right. I shouldn't have done what I did. I wanted to tell you—I tried a hundred times. I just couldn't because I was afraid I'd lose you. I fell for you, Antonio."

I had hoped my confession would soften him. Maybe allow him to forgive me. It didn't.

"Tell your *family* that I'll be back at work," he said in a tight voice. "I need the job, as you know."

Then he slammed the door in my face.

"Mea culpa," I whispered as tears stung my eyes. *I'm so very sorry.*

But it was too late.

Seventeen

Antonio

BETRAYAL!
   Standing in our kitchen, watching butter melt in the pan, I felt like my life had turned into a tragic opera. Just when it was beginning to be all that I wanted.

I was seriously angry. I had never felt this betrayed. Not even when my papa died.

I had been totally wrong about Americans. Yes, they were rich, selfish, spoiled—but more, they were deceptive!

I tossed onions and peppers into the pan. If Carrie—Carrie. How American that sounded! If Carrie had waited five more minutes to knock on the door, we might have had a repeat of her first visit to my house. My burning the vegetables I had meant to sauté.

I thought about the way she'd helped me clean

the house—a house she didn't live in. The way she had handled my sisters.

I remembered her working in the restaurant. I had thought she was such a hard worker. But it was all games. Games designed to teach me a lesson. Well, I'd learned a lesson, all right. I'd never again trust another American.

"Antonio, when will supper be ready?" Mara asked.

I stirred the onions and peppers. "Soon."

Mara hopped onto a stool. "When is your friend coming back to see us?"

"What friend?" I asked.

"Carrina! I really liked her," she announced.

"Her name is Carrie, and she's never coming back to see us," I responded.

"Why?"

"Because she's an American," I explained. Because she was dishonest. Because she had stabbed me in the heart.

"What's wrong with Americans?" Mara asked.

I glanced at Mara. Most Italians didn't mind Americans. They loved tourists, loved showing off their country. If I didn't have to wait on them, I probably wouldn't mind them either. I didn't want Mara to dislike them.

"There's nothing wrong with Americans." I moved to the counter and sat on the stool beside her. "The problem is Carrie. She made me think she was Italian."

"How did she *make* you think it?" Mara asked.

Ah, to be young and unable to understand so much. "Well," I began, "she didn't really make me think it, I suppose. I just assumed she was Italian because she spoke Italian, she looks Italian, and when I told her that I wanted to meet the Year Abroad student, she didn't tell me that she was the Year Abroad student."

Mara's blue eyes widened. "Carrina's the Year Abroad student?"

"Yes," I admitted.

She giggled. "So you wanted to meet someone you already knew."

"Sort of. Only I didn't know that I knew her."

She stared at me. "So if you wanted to meet the Year Abroad student and she was the Year Abroad student, why can't she come over?"

I slumped on the stool. "Because she lied to me—by omission. By not telling me, she deceived me."

"Oh." Mara stuck out her bottom lip. "I liked her," she repeated.

"I liked her too." Had fallen for too, as a matter of fact, but she wasn't the girl I thought she was.

"Antonio, what's that stink?" Mara asked.

I groaned and rushed back to the stove. My diced onions and peppers were burned to a crisp. Fortunately I had more this time that I could cut and cook.

My gaze slid to the celery stalk. I thought of my fencing match with Carrina—Carrie. Funny how I suddenly realized that "Carrie" suited her. Short and quick. Energetic, even.

Just like Mara, I liked Carrie too. But it wasn't enough. Not when she'd betrayed me.

School became a nightmare.

Everywhere I looked, there was Carrie.

I must have been the only person in the entire school who hadn't met her. Only I *had* met her. I just hadn't realized that I'd met her.

Whenever our paths crossed, our eyes locked. Mine hard. Hers . . . sad. I should have felt glad about that. Felt a measure of satisfaction, but I didn't. When I couldn't stand it any longer, I approached her in the hallway.

"Are you deliberately getting in my way now?" I demanded.

"No, before I was deliberately avoiding you." She gave me a wry smile. "You know. By ducking into boys' bathrooms."

"You went into the boys' bathroom to avoid seeing me?" I asked.

"I didn't realize it was the boys' bathroom. I just knew it was a door and you were getting close. At the time I didn't think anything would be worse than you finding out that I was American," she explained.

"And now?" I insisted.

"I was right. There was nothing worse."

I should have felt a measure of satisfaction. Instead I wanted to draw her into my arms and find a way to get that sad look off her face.

I turned on my heel and headed for my next

class. No way was I going to comfort her. No way would I ever forgive her.

I would despise her as long as I remembered her.

Unfortunately, I feared I would remember her forever.

Eighteen

Carrie

EVENING WAS BEGINNING to descend. I sat on the balcony outside my bedroom and stared—at nothing. Not even the incredible sunset could stir me. Being miserable was not how I'd planned to spend my year in Rome. How had my whole world crashed?

I was staying away from La Sera. I'd stopped dodging Antonio at school. There was no point in doing that anymore. Except that it hurt so much to see him. Our paths crossed constantly. I absolutely couldn't believe that I'd managed to avoid him for so long. *I'd make a great spy,* I thought.

I'd e-mailed Dana and Robin about the situation; their advice was to keep trying, to keep apologizing and explaining myself and pray he'd forgive me. I wasn't sure he would forgive me. In fact, I was sure he wouldn't.

I propped my bare feet on the wrought-iron railing and tapped my pencil against the legal pad resting on my thighs. I still had to come up with a "lesson plan" for the English class. Then I'd have to go into the class—where I knew Antonio would be waiting—stand up in front of everyone, and explain what *hey, dude,* and *going postal* meant. I really wanted to give them an American experience, but the experience encompassed so much. Where to begin? I hadn't a clue.

I heard a shuffling sound and glanced over my shoulder. Elena stepped onto the balcony and dropped down. She folded her legs beneath her and leaned back against the brick wall. She peered up at me. "Are you avoiding my English class?" she asked in English.

I smiled. "Yep."

She wrinkled her nose. "*Yep.* Is that like *yes?*"

"Yep," I repeated. "Sometimes we say *yeah* or *uh-huh* or *you bet.*"

"But *no* is just *no,* right?" she inquired.

"Nope. No could be *uh-uh* or *nah* or *no way,*" I explained. I rolled my hands one over the other. "And American is more than just words. How do I explain chicken-fried steak, home fries, and Texas toast? Pictures are so boring—I wanted students to see the real thing, but how am I going to take food to school? If there was a kitchen at the school, I could offer to cook for the class." I drew a big *X* on the yellow paper. "No matter how I try to present this information, it's going to put every student in that class to sleep."

Elena sat up straighter. "What if we had a party here?"

I stared at her. "A party."

She smiled brightly. "Yep. Saturday evening. We could invite all of the students in Signora Calendri's classes. She probably has about fifty. It would be crowded, but I think it would be great fun. Then you could cook your fried-chicken steak," she said, her eyes sparkling.

I laughed. "Chicken-fried steak." I gnawed on my lower lip. The idea really appealed to me. And with all of the English classes here, I wouldn't have to stand in front of a room, trying to avoid looking at Antonio. "We could have a Texas theme," I suggested, really getting into the idea. "I could make invitations that say, 'Y'all come see us, ya hear?'"

Elena giggled. "When you don't talk Italian, you really sound funny."

"You mean my Texas drawl?" I asked, really emphasizing my twang.

"Yep," she said, beaming.

"You should hear my friend Robin," I told her. "She has a really heavy accent." Unless her time in London had tempered it. But I couldn't really see that happening. How could a few weeks erase sixteen years of good-ole-boy talkin'?

I ripped off the top sheet of paper—my *X*'ed paper. I started to make a list. "I have some home videos I can

154

show." I glanced at Elena. "Seeing my brothers will really give the students a taste of Texas life."

"I think you should wear one of your Texas outfits that I've seen in your closet. Maybe I should wear one too," Elena hinted. "Just to give everyone a true feeling for Texas."

"Good idea," I admitted. My list grew. Food, exhibits, videos, music. I'd brought some Dixie Chicks and Clay Walker CDs. Some 'N Sync and Backstreet Boys as well, but I figured I should really play country music. Everything I wanted to do was snowballing.

"Do you think Signora Calendri would mind if I put the lesson off for a week?" I asked. "There's so much I need to do to have everything the way I want it."

"I think she will think it's worth the wait," Elena stated.

"I'll talk with her tomorrow," I murmured. But my excitement was mounting. I could share a part of my culture . . . and maybe when Antonio got a true taste of Texas hospitality, he might forgive me a little.

The next week at school, when I saw Antonio in the hallway, I called out to him. "Antonio!"

He stopped walking and turned. My heart pounded as I approached him. I couldn't help but think that he looked so totally hot. And so totally still angry.

"Did Signora Calendri give you an invitation to

the Deep in the Heart of Texas party?" I dared to ask.

"Yes, but I have to work Saturday," he said without emotion.

"We'll be partying late. You could come by after work—you know, to unwind," I suggested.

I watched as his jaw clenched.

"You wanted to learn about Americans," I began.

"You've already taught me everything I need to know about Americans," he interrupted.

He turned on his heel and walked away.

No, I thought, *I didn't teach you anything about Americans. I only taught you something about me.*

Nineteen

Antonio

LATE SATURDAY AFTERNOON I arrived at La Sera, not at all in the mood to work. I stood at the back of the kitchen, looking at the invitation to Carrie's party.

She'd drawn a Texas flag on the front. Inside she'd written, *Y'all come on over for a good time and good food—Texas style.* The party started at seven at Elena's. At Elena's. I shook my head. How had I managed to miss the fact that Elena Pietra was hosting this year's Year Abroad student? I felt like I had buried myself in a cocoon—until Carrie with her exuberance had made me want to do things again.

It had taken a lot of courage for her to approach me in the hall. I hated to admit that fact because it made me feel like I should admire her. She had looked sad when she'd talked to me. I was glad she was suffering. It was only fair that she should hurt the way I hurt.

No, I thought, I really didn't want her to hurt. I just wanted her to stay out of my life.

"Antonio?"

At Roberto's summons I stuffed the invitation into my pocket and turned. It was time to get to work.

"Good news." Roberto smiled. "Papa just called, and we're closing the restaurant for the night."

"Closing?" I sounded like an echo.

"Yep, but you'll still get paid as though it had remained open," Roberto assured me. "Carrina's having her party tonight, and Mama and Papa want the family to be able to go over there. Apparently Carrina thought it would be nice to cook a meal for everyone. Mama and Papa went to help." He grinned. "She's giving them a crash course in cooking Texas cuisine. So let's close up, and you can ride over there with me and my brothers."

I shook my head. "I'll help you close up, but I'm not going to the party."

"Why do you have such a problem with Carrina?" he asked.

I thought my eyes were going to pop out of my head. "I can't believe you asked me that. Don't you know what she did?"

Roberto shrugged. "Sure, I know. We all know. As far as I'm concerned, though, you deserved what she did."

"Deserved it? Are you out of your mind?" I cried.

"No. I'm very sane. You, however, have a chip on your shoulder the size of a Roman hill. You come very close to being rude to our American customers. Is it any wonder they're rude back?"

"I'm rude?" I asked.

"Yeah, you're always looking down on them. The only reason Papa doesn't fire you is because he knows you need the job. You liked Carrina just fine when you thought she was Italian. She's the same girl."

"No, she's not. She's an American," I pointed out.

Roberto glared at me. "Antonio, she was an American all along."

I did not want to see Carrie. But I had to admit that I was a little curious about what she would share with everyone.

All right. Maybe I wanted to see her a little bit.

With Carrie's cousins, I arrived at Elena's. Elena opened the door. Smiling brightly, she said in English, "Y'all come on in."

She ushered us into the house and closed the door behind us. Her eyes widened slightly when she spotted me in the group, but she didn't say anything about my being there.

"Come on into the kitchen," she said. "We're cooking bebarcue chicken."

I heard Carrie's laughter. "Elena, that's barbecue chicken!" she shouted from the kitchen.

Elena waved her hands in the air. "Whatever. Y'all come help."

I hung back as Carrie's cousins followed Elena into the kitchen. I heard cries of hello and then Carrie's voice as she rapidly gave orders.

Slowly I approached the kitchen and peered inside through the open arched doorway. What an incredible mess!

All except Carrie. She wore tight-fitting blue jeans, a cowboy-looking shirt, boots, a cowboy hat, and a vest. Did she really wear those clothes back home?

"What is this?" Roberto asked as he lifted a ladle and poured thick white goo back into the pot.

"That," Carrie told him, "is white cream gravy. You pour it over the chicken-fried steak that Uncle Vito is cooking. If it's made right, it's guaranteed to clog your heart."

She looked so happy with her family. So relaxed. She hadn't spotted me yet. I didn't know if I really wanted her to. She was just like the girl I'd fallen in love with—only she wasn't.

I heard a knock on the door. Everyone in the kitchen was talking at once, so no one else heard it. I figured it was probably students from class arriving early. I thought it would be all right if I let them in.

I crossed back to the door and opened it. Four people stood there. I'd never seen them before. A tall, English-looking guy with blond hair had his arm around a blond girl. Beside them was a girl with short red hair and a tall, dark-haired guy. All four were smiling like lunatics. None of them looked Italian.

"Ciao!" the blond girl said with an accent that could have come right out of an American western.

"Robin, I thought *ciao* meant 'good-bye,'" the redhead said with an accent similar to her friend's but not quite as bad.

"Actually, Dana, I believe it means both," the blond guy said. I'd been right: The guy was British.

"Kit, are you telling us that Italians have one word that means two different things?" Robin asked.

"I believe so," Kit said.

"Just hold on a minute," Dana said. "Let me pull out my trusty English–Italian dictionary." She reached into her purse.

"I speak a little English," I told them.

The girls' eyes widened. "Wonderful!" they both said at once.

"I love Italians!" Dana said. "You're so much friendlier than the French."

Things were starting to click. Carrie had told me that her two best friends were in the Year Abroad program. One in London. One in Paris. It didn't hit me until now that they were Americans and not Italians.

"That's because the French don't like Americans," the dark-haired guy said. It was the first time he'd spoken. Definitely American.

"Alex is right about that," Dana said. "But right now that's not important. What is important is that we're Carrie's friends, and we're here!" She glanced quickly around. "If this is the right house."

161

I don't know why I smiled. "It is. Come in."

"*Grazie,*" Robin said with such a twang that she mutilated the word. She held up a hand. "That means 'thank you,' and that's all it means."

They walked into the house.

"I smell barbecue!" Dana yelled.

I closed the door and turned just in time to see Carrie dash out of the kitchen. Her mouth dropped open, and tears filled her eyes. "Oh my gosh! What are y'all doing here?"

Y'all? Did they really say y'all in Texas? I wondered. I figured Carrie had written it on the invitation as some sort of joke and Elena had been in on the joke.

Robin and Dana rushed forward, and the three girls hugged.

"I can't believe y'all are here!" Carrie leaned back. "How did you get here?"

"Well," Robin began, "Kit and I took the Channel Tunnel rail service from London to Paris. There we met up with Dana and Alex. And we all took the French train. It goes one hundred and eighty-five miles an hour." She snapped her fingers. "We were out of France in no time."

"We arrived in Italy," Dana continued. "Got on an Italian train, and, as they say, 'All roads lead to Rome.' We knew you were nervous, and we wanted to be here to offer moral support."

Nervous? I couldn't imagine Carrie nervous.

"Nervous?" Carrie questioned. "Try terrified. A week ago this sounded like such a good idea . . .

162

and now . . . now . . ." She gave them a smile that transformed her face into one of rare beauty. "Now I know I can pull it off."

She looked past them to the guys. "I can't believe y'all came too."

"I wouldn't miss an opportunity to see Robin charm people with her accent," Kit said.

Carrie hugged him. "Some big brother you turned out to be."

"I fancy the role of boyfriend more," he admitted.

Then she turned to Alex. "Alex Turner Johnson. We were in Mr. Martin's math class together."

He gave her a crooked grin. "Right."

Then she hugged him too. "It's good to see a familiar face."

When she stepped back, her gaze fell on me. The sparkle left her eyes, and her smile withered like a flower that went too long without water. "Antonio," she rasped. "I didn't know you were here."

I shrugged. "I came with your cousins."

She pointed to the people surrounding her. "You met my friends."

I nodded.

"Everyone, this is Antonio," she said softly.

"Jolly good to meet you," Kit said.

"Yeah, nice to meet you, dude," Alex said.

But Dana and Robin apparently knew more about me than either of the guys did because they were just staring at me as though I were a bug they were considering squashing and they couldn't figure out why I was here. Even I wasn't sure why I was here.

"Carrina!" Signore Romano yelled. "I don't know what to do with this food."

Carrie jumped and then looked at her friends. "Kitchen duty awaits."

"We'll help," Dana said.

I watched Carrie and her friends disappear into the kitchen. I leaned against the door. Signore Romano had closed the trattoria so his family would be here to help Carrie. Sure, she was his niece, but not having the restaurant open tonight was going to cost him a fortune. Her friends had traveled from two different countries to be with her during this event. She apparently instilled loyalty in family and friends.

Maybe I needed to take another look at Carrie Giovani.

Things got really crazy after all the students in Signora Calendri's English classes arrived. I figured there were close to fifty people crowded into the Pietra home.

The restaurant had the capacity to hold 160 patrons. But fifty people crammed in a house weren't nearly as organized as 160 people sitting in a restaurant. For one thing, the Pietra family had only one table and four chairs.

So people stood around in the kitchen and the front room. Eating, talking, laughing. I'd sampled chicken-fried steak smothered in cream gravy—according to the folded card in front of it—home fries, Texas toast, barbecue chicken, baked beans, and corn bread. I thought the chicken-fried steak was especially good. I even considered getting the recipe so I could make it sometime for my sisters.

Of course, the person with the recipe was the person who I really didn't want to talk to. I certainly wouldn't ask her for anything.

Carrie's extravaganza had one rule. Everyone had to speak English. Made sense. After all, we were here because we were taking English as our foreign language. It was funny listening to people stammer and stutter with unfamiliar phrases.

But Carrie never laughed. Sometimes her smile was a little brighter when she corrected people or told them an alternate way to say what they wanted. And she made them laugh with words and phrases that we'd never heard in class: *boot scootin'*, *yeehaw, heck fire*.

Her friends were teaching as well. They all had incredible accents. And they really did say y'all. I heard them saying it constantly, and it was obvious that it just slipped out. It wasn't part of any grand scheme to make us think they said words that they didn't.

"Okay," Carrie announced. "I've got my video camera set up in the *salotto* so I can show you Texas. It's gonna be a tight squeeze, so be sure you sit by someone you like."

Everyone laughed as they made their way into the *salotto*. As I had most of the night, I held back. I thought about going home, but unfortunately my curiosity was stronger.

I crept to the doorway and peered into the room. Carrie stood at the front beside the television. She'd hooked her video camera to the television and was playing the video so everyone could see it.

"This is my high school's football team," Carrie explained as guys in purple uniforms started running toward guys in white uniforms. "The Mustangs. Friday night is football night, and in Texas football is everything."

The camera zoomed in on the people watching the games. There was Carrie sitting between Dana and Robin. I wondered if she'd ever had a boyfriend. If maybe he was on the football team. She jumped up and started yelling for some guy named Biff to go.

I didn't like the jealousy I felt at the thought that this guy might mean something to her—now or in the past.

"My dad closes down the pizzeria during the game—but after the game!" Carrie's voice trailed off, and the scene changed. "My dad's pizzeria," she explained. "My brother Marcus has the camera—anything to get out of work."

I watched her carrying pitchers of soft drinks to tables. Every now and then she'd stop by a table where Robin and Dana were eating pizza. They'd talk for a while, and then she'd rush off to get

166

someone else's pizza or drinks. The scene changed to the kitchen, and the camera zoomed in on a rotund man flipping pizza crusts in the air.

Signora Romano shouted, "That's my brother!"

There was a little break in the video, and we were looking at another stadium, but it looked very different from that of the football game.

"Now, this is a rodeo," Carrie explained. "My dad has the camera." The camera swept along the seats. Dana and Robin were there. Then she pointed to her sister and four of her brothers. "Now, believe it or not, this is how guys in Mustang have fun. You're going to see my oldest brother, Marcus, riding a bull."

"Riding a bull" seemed to be giving her brother a lot more credit than he deserved. The bull crashed out of the gate. It did a couple of kicks. Marcus hit the ground, scrambled to his feet, ran to a fence, and climbed over.

"The whole family is hoping someday a bull will knock some sense into him," she explained, and everyone laughed.

The video continued to play, and Carrie continued to explain life at her home, but I'd seen enough. I'd seen that her enthusiasm wasn't something that she'd discovered in Rome. I'd seen that she worked hard and played hard. Whether she was in Texas or Rome, Carrie Giovani embraced life to the fullest. That was one of the reasons I'd fallen so hard for her. She did everything with such excitement.

Except now when our paths crossed, the excitement was missing. I wasn't going to feel guilty about that. I wasn't the one who had decided to teach someone a lesson. I wandered back to the front room.

Carrie had set some things on the table. A book that seemed to be a history of her school. Pictures of students, students in class, students engaged in sports. She had a map of Texas showing Mustang, her hometown. It was just a dot on the map.

A CD player was playing music low. Some women were singing that Earl had to die. The sentiment seemed strange, but I liked the beat of the music. I guessed this was the kind of music Carrie listened to at home.

"I didn't think you were going to come," a soft voice said behind me.

I stiffened. Then I forced myself to relax, turn around slowly, and face Carrie. "I was just curious."

"If you have any questions, I'll be happy to answer them," she murmured, but she looked anything but happy.

I considered blowing her off, telling her again that I had all the answers, but watching that video had caused me to wonder about a few things. It would be silly to let my disappointment over what she'd done interfere with my learning. Besides, who knew what questions might appear on my English exam?

"Don't you resent that your friends don't have to work?" I asked, remembering how they'd been laughing and eating pizza while she'd been rushing around her dad's restaurant.

She laughed. "Robin lives on a farm. While I'm sleeping, Robin is milking cows at five in the morning. I'm a night owl. I wouldn't trade places with her for the world. And poor Dana works in a clothing store. The stories she tells about women squeezing a size-sixteen body into a size-eight dress. No thanks. I'll take my dad's restaurant any day."

"The guys who came with them," I began.

"They're Robin's and Dana's boyfriends," she interrupted. "Kit is Robin's host brother while she's in London. They sorta decided they weren't really interested in a brother-sister relationship. Alex is from Mustang. He's a Year Abroad student as well. He's in Paris. He and Dana hooked up. I'm sure he'd be happy to answer your questions if you'd like to know America from a guy's point of view."

I shook my head, but I was curious about something else. "You told Robin and Dana about me."

Her cheeks burned bright red as she nodded. "Yeah. Like I told you before, I can tell them the worst thing about me . . . and right now that just happens to involve you."

"Why didn't you tell me that you were an American?" I asked.

I watched as she gnawed on her lower lip and the sadness in her eyes increased. "I wanted to teach you a lesson, but by the time I realized that you didn't deserve the lesson—I liked you too much and knew if you found out the truth, you'd stop liking me."

"I told you that I wanted to meet the Year Abroad student," I reminded her.

"Yeah, and you also told me that Americans were silly and selfish. And as it turns out, you were right. I'm really sorry about that." She slipped her fingers underneath the chain at her throat and lifted the necklace I'd given her over her head. "I'm sure you want this back."

I really didn't want it back. But I let her drop it into my palm, and I closed my fingers around it. I could feel the heat from her body on the medallion. I still wanted it to protect her, but I didn't seem able to find the words that would allow me to give it back to her. I tugged on the ring she'd given me. She touched my hand, and I stilled.

"Keep it," she ordered. "Maybe it'll remind you that life is a puzzle, and it isn't always easy to figure out how it works." Then she pointed toward the kitchen. "There's some apple pie on the counter in there. Give it a try. It's as American as you can get."

I watched her walk back to the family room. Someone stopped her, and they started to talk.

Carrie had said she was sorry. I was sorry too. More than I would have thought humanly possible. Because the truth was, in spite of everything, I still adored her.

Twenty

Carrie

"I STILL CAN'T believe that y'all are really here!" I exclaimed.

I was sitting on my bed, my back against the headboard, my knees pressed to my chest, and my arms wrapped around my legs. Dana and Robin sat at the foot of my bed—just like they had a hundred times before in Mustang.

Dana shrugged. "We just thought that you needed us."

They were definitely the best friends in the whole world. Once the party had ended and everyone had left, I'd discovered that they'd been in contact with Aunt Bianca. She'd helped them arrange things—getting here in time and finding Elena's house. Aunt Bianca had even talked with Signora Pietra, and she had agreed they could spend the night here. An American slumber party in Rome. We'd invited Elena to join us, but she said she'd had enough Texas for the evening.

Alex and Kit were spending the night with my cousins. They would no doubt have stories to tell on their trip home tomorrow.

But tonight I was happier than I'd been in a long time.

"You both look so good in love," I teased, butchering a line from a George Strait song. "I can't believe that Alex and Kit came too."

Dana blushed. "Well, actually, Alex came because he wants to see the Colosseum tomorrow before we leave. He has this thing about the movie *Gladiator,* and he just thought it would be awesome to see the arena."

I smiled. "I don't know, Dana. I saw the way he looked at you all night. I think he would have come even if there was no Colosseum." I shook my head. "I didn't remember Alex Turner Johnson being so cute."

Dana grinned like someone who was completely in love. "He turned out to be quite a surprise."

"Even if he isn't French?" Robin asked.

"Especially since he isn't French," Dana confirmed.

"And what about you and Kit?" I asked Robin.

"It's kinda neat having your boyfriend living right across the hall," Robin admitted.

Dana cleared her throat. "I was surprised Antonio was here."

"Yeah, he told me that he wasn't going to come." I wrinkled my brow. "Well, he said he had to work, but my uncle closed the trattoria, so . . . I don't know. I guess Antonio decided what the heck."

"He's really hot looking," Robin pointed out.

"Tell me about it. That's one of the reasons I fell for him—a major mistake."

"I don't know," Dana said thoughtfully. "Every time I looked at him, he was watching you."

"Not the way that Alex watches you, though. For Antonio it's more like, how do I hate thee, let me count the ways." I'd just butchered the lines from a poem. Seemed like I was butchering everything in my life: songs, poems, my love for Antonio, his for me.

"I don't think what you did was so awful," Robin stated.

"Yeah, it wasn't so awful," Dana seconded.

That was what best friends were for.

On Sunday afternoon I felt like a fifth wheel as we toured the Colosseum. Kit and Robin were so obviously in love. So were Dana and Alex. They held hands and sneaked kisses whenever they thought no one was looking.

I was 110 percent happy for my friends. I really was. But I had no hand to hold. No one to share this monumental Colosseum with. No one whispering in my ear and making me laugh.

The design of the Colosseum was truly amazing. I'd

always thought it was circular, but it was actually shaped like an ellipse. We were walking along an internal corridor. It was wide, designed to allow large, unruly crowds to get to their seats within ten minutes. We could use these corridors at the stadium in Mustang.

We'd just been to the underground area where animals had been kept in days of old. Their cages were actually elevators that lifted them to the arena level when it was their turn to fight. Pretty impressive—if you were into the gory sports of our ancestors.

We walked through an arched entrance. There were eighty that had allowed spectators into the seating area. We followed another path until we reached the arena.

"I can actually hear the clash of swords," Alex said quietly.

I had to admit there was an eerie cadence in the air.

"I can see the bright red blood," Dana whispered in awe.

"I can envision the madness of the crowds," Kit admitted.

Robin looked at me. "I see sand and stone."

"Same here," I concurred, not wanting her to feel unimaginative. Although I could also see the emperor sitting in the podium with his wealthiest and most loyal subjects. I briefly pictured myself sitting there. Nah, I decided I'd rather be a female gladiator. Although rare, they had existed. I thought of my fencing match with Antonio. Celery had worked well as a rapier, but I wasn't certain what vegetable I'd use as a broadsword.

"I see Antonio," Robin murmured.

I leaned forward, certain I'd misheard her. In London, Robin had taken to talking really softly so no one would detect her accent. But I couldn't figure out why she was doing that here. "What did you say?"

"Antonio," she repeated, barely moving her lips. "One hundred and eighty degrees."

"My Antonio?" I rasped.

She nodded slightly.

"What's he doing here?" I whispered.

"Watching you," she muttered.

My heart pounded as I slowly turned. My gaze clashed with Antonio's. I could hear the hiss of steel sword sliding against steel sword. Only I didn't want to fight with him anymore, or argue, or apologize.

He stood within an entrance, his arms folded over his chest. Watching. Waiting. For what?

He started walking toward me. I thought I knew how those in the arena had felt when the lions were let loose.

"Kit, let's go explore," Robin said. Out of the corner of my eye I saw her take Kit's hand and stroll away.

I wanted to call her back. *Don't leave me,* my mind screamed.

"Oh my gosh," Dana declared. "What's he doing here?"

"I don't know," I answered.

"Well, Alex and I are just going to tiptoe out of

earshot. Holler if you need us," she told me.

It took every ounce of willpower I possessed not to grab her arm and jerk her to my side. Some friends they were turning out to be . . . leaving me alone.

I thought about retreating. But Italians had stood within the center of the Colosseum and faced things more frightening than an angry guy.

I took a deep breath, squared my shoulders, and decided I'd apologized enough.

"Sight-seeing?" I croaked when Antonio stopped inches away from me.

A corner of his mouth lifted. "Not exactly. I overheard Alex tell Kit last night that he planned to come here today. I assumed you'd welcome the opportunity to check off the page in your guidebook."

I nodded. "Yeah, I haven't been doing much sight-seeing lately, so I figured today would be a good day to start catching up."

I realized that he'd figured out I would be here—but that still didn't explain what he was doing here. I wrinkled my brow. "So what are you doing here? I know that you hate me, so why in the world would you come here, knowing that I was going to be here?"

"I don't hate you, Carrie," he said solemnly.

"I don't hate you" was a long way from "I still like you so much" . . . but still, it gave me a spark of hope that we could at least be friends.

"I'm glad you don't hate me, Antonio," I confessed. "I truly never meant to hurt you. I just thought . . . I don't know; I just thought—"

"That I had misjudged Americans," he interrupted.

"Yeah. I mean, if you could get to know Dana and Robin, you'd realize that some Americans are the most wonderful people to be around," I explained.

He took a step closer. "You're right. I noticed last night. Your friends. Their boyfriends. Doing everything they could to help you."

Now I understood. It was like a lightbulb was suddenly turned on in my head. He'd mentioned countless times that he wanted to get to know an American, and I had three great examples right here.

"They're only going to be here a couple more hours, but if you want to get to know them better, I'm sure they won't mind if you join them. And I'll even bug out—"

"Bug out?" he repeated.

"Leave. Since you dislike me, I don't want to interfere with you getting to know them," I responded.

"I don't dislike you, Carrie. That's the problem. I want to dislike you, I really do . . . but I just can't."

A spark of hope filled my heart like a star shooting across the vast Texas sky.

"Maybe we could start over," I suggested.

He shook his head. "If we start over, I'd have to forget everything."

My heart plummeted as I realized that Antonio wanted to gnaw on my betrayal like a scroungy dog with a bone. I blinked, trying to stop the tears from stinging my eyes. "I understand."

"I don't think you do." He lifted the chain from around his neck and slowly settled it around mine until the medallion rested at the base of my throat. "If we started over, I'd have to forget the way your hand feels in mine. The sound of your laughter, the warmth of your smiles."

My heart was pounding a mile a minute as he took my hand and pulled me toward him. "I think it's better to remember so I don't forget that American girls are smart, work hard, and aren't selfish. And that I'm a little stupid."

"You're not stupid," I said breathlessly.

"Yes, I am. I listened to my pride instead of my heart—and almost lost you."

He lowered his mouth to mine and kissed me deeply. Ah, I liked the way his heart spoke.

I wound my arms around his neck, and he pulled me closer. The kiss was fantastic. I allowed myself to accept it and fall into it, like diving into the deep end of a heated pool.

This time there was nothing between us but the truth. My knees grew weak. Antonio was kissing Carrie—the American. My heart soared.

He drew back and met my gaze. "I like you so much, Carrie. So much."

My smile was so big that I thought my jaws would crack. "You know, Carrina is my real name. And I sure like the way you say it."

"Carrina," he repeated in a low voice.

I pressed my hand against his chest and felt the

rapid beating of his heart. "I like you so much too, Antonio. I have for so long. Honestly, I didn't mean to deceive—"

He touched his finger to my lips. "The only thing that matters is that you love me." He trailed his finger around my face. "You're a puzzle, Carrina, and I intend to spend the next year figuring you out. And if a year isn't long enough, I have a pocketful of coins that you can toss into the Trevi Fountain to ensure you return to Rome."

Joy shot through me. Antonio settled his lips against mine, and I became immersed in the kiss. Totally. Completely.

I was vaguely aware that within the shadows cast by the Colosseum, Robin was kissing Kit, and Dana was kissing Alex.

Our year abroad had only just begun. But already I knew that it was going to be the best year of my life.

Do you ever wonder about falling in love? About members of the opposite sex? Do you need a little friendly advice but have no one to turn to? Well, that's where we come in . . . Jenny and Jake. Send us those questions you're dying to ask, and we'll give you the straight scoop on life and love.

DEAR JAKE

Q: *When my crush found out I liked him, he stopped talking to me. We used to be friends, and now he totally ignores me. What should I do?*

TP, Omaha, NE

A: This is a toughie because it involves you having to take a risk. The only way to find out why he's giving you the cold shoulder is to ask him—straight out. You might be surprised at his answer. Just because he's ignoring you doesn't necessarily mean he doesn't like you back. Guys do things for reasons that girls would never guess. Shyness and insecurity are two major ones!

Q: *What do guys look for in a girl? I have a crush on a guy named Mark, and I want to do whatever I can to make him like me back.*

SJ, Hayti, MO

A: Since there's no way to make someone like you, there's only one thing you can do: Be yourself. Yeah, yeah, I know, you've heard that before. But being yourself means that you celebrate everything that makes you *you*. Whether you're loud or quiet, serious or silly, into rap or country music, whatever, you're *you*. And *you* are all you need to attract someone!

DEAR JENNY

Q: *Help! My parents caught me and my boyfriend making out, and now they're threatening to send me away to camp for the summer. My parents say they're doing it for my own good and that Steve and I are too serious too soon. Can you print an answer that'll tell them they're wrong?*

LF, Rockville, MD

A: The only person who can change your parents' minds is you. Clearly they're worried. Perhaps you could sit down with your folks and tell them how you feel, that you don't want to go to camp, that you want to be near your boyfriend, that you want their trust. Start the dialogue and see what happens. Your parents just might surprise you with how reasonable they can be.

Q: *My best friend is getting on my nerves. All she talks about is her boyfriend. And that's when she even has time to talk to me in the first place. She's always with him. I'm really mad at her. Should I tell her to choose—me or him? I'm really worried she'd pick him.*

GS, Branford, CT

A: Ultimatums usually backfire—so I don't suggest asking her to choose. What I do suggest is letting her know how you feel. What you really seem to be saying is that you miss the friendship. I'll bet she does too, even if she's on planet Boyfriend these days.

Do you have any questions about love?
Although we can't respond individually to your letters,
you just might find your questions answered in our column.

Write to:

Jenny Burgess or Jake Korman

c/o 17th Street Productions,

an Alloy Online, Inc. company.

33 West 17th Street
New York, NY 10011

Don't miss any of the books in *Love Stories*
—the romantic series from Bantam Books!

Francine Pascal's
SVH

senioryear

You're watching
"Dawson's Creek"...

You're wearing
Urban Decay...

Have you read
senioryear?

Bantam

www.sweetvalley.com

BFYR 232

You'll always remember your first love.

Looking for signs he's ready to fall in love?

Want the guy's point of view?

Then you should check out *Love Stories*. Romantic stories that tell it like it is—why he doesn't call, how to ask him out, when to say good-bye.

Available wherever books are sold.

www.randomhouse.com

BFYR 209